AGAINST THE WIND

Jane-Claire's Personal Salvation

DAWN C CROUCH

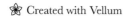 Created with Vellum

Many Thanks and Much Love to My husband, Steve

and our children

Kelly, Dominique, Stephen and Caroline.

ONE

Usual Preparations

Sunday morning and the doors to the church are locked. They should have known.

Fifteen-year-old Jane-Claire Stevens stands with her family at the main entrance of the modern steel and cement monolith located across the street from the beach.

Mason, her dad, tries a second time to pull the doors open. Nothing. They don't even budge.

The family stands, waits.

"I've never heard of such a thing." Dona, Jane-Claire's mom who insists on regular attendance, paces the steps. She did her job, rousting everyone out of bed that morning with coffee and sausage biscuits, a winning combo that can't be refused.

"Wait. Beep the car for me. I've got to film this." Jane-Claire runs down the steps toward the family's Ford Expedition.

Mason presses the keyless entry.

"The parking lot's empty. It's a dead giveaway." Jane-Claire twirls in a lone patch of bright sunshine gracing the middle of the circular drive.

Lerue, her brother, rubs his eyes. He is not quite awake yet. "I just thought we were early."

Jane-Claire returns from the SUV with her prize video camera in hand. She documents the phenomena of the cancelled church service then captures building waves on the beach. Layers of clouds in the skyscape high above her twist together and tear apart.

Her family lives in Gulfport, a beautiful little town on the Mississippi Gulf coast.

Their beach cottage is on Second Street, only a block off of the ritzier Beach Highway studded by antebellum homes. Small and old, their home is considered safe since it didn't flood during Hurricane Camille, one of the only Category 5 hurricanes to ever hit the continental United States.

The family moved to Gulfport because of her parents' dream to settle where they honeymooned.

Phase one is now. Her dad works in the emergency department at the big hospital. He plans to staff the hospital's urgent care centers when he gets older, phase two complete.

Her parents think that if they live at the beach, then Lerue and she will visit more often in their hypothetical futures when they have their own families. Lerue and Jane-Claire haven't thought that far ahead.

"I guess all the restaurants are closed too." Lerue trudges down the steps to their premiere parking space. Seriously. They should have called before leaving the house.

"White Cap is open." Jane-Claire waits for him in the circle drive. "I saw it on the way over. They put 'Welcome Jim Cantore and the Weather Channel' on their sign out front."

"Then let's get some po-boys and go home. We need to

board up and finish taking the lawn furniture in before I go to work." Mason shakes his head at what he now perceives as a waste of valuable time and gets in the car.

As they drive down the Beach Highway, he points out the former site of his Grandfather's home in Long Beach.

Mason spent most of his summers as a boy with his Pappy. Built by a sea captain, he details how the house had thick ship windows, port holes, and minimal damage during Camille, but was sold and bulldozed anyway. Dad has a long history on the coast.

Jane-Claire always listens when they drive by but all she ever sees is an empty lot.

Today, she notices that the people in the small house that's more of a camp next door are packing their car. Their house windows are already boarded.

The po-boys at White Cap are great; overstuffed with shrimp and dressed with loads of shredded lettuce and home grown tomatoes. Despite the sign out front, the Weather Channel crew is nowhere in sight. In fact, no one else is in the restaurant which makes for zero conversation and a quick meal.

Jane-Claire gives half of her sandwich to Lerue. Dona wraps some biscuits in a napkin.

Mason tips the waitress with his emergency money, a fifty dollar bill tucked in the back of his wallet. The waitress locks the door as soon as the Stevens family leaves.

The beach in Gulfport is broad and flat, great for walks, skim boarding, and picnics. Lerue skims every day after school so Mason and Dona never worry about their son playing too many video games. Lerue is hardly ever inside the house. His only concern is who is the best skim boarder, and how he can teach the newbies to be better.

The water off the beach is shallow and murky because barrier islands with names like Cat and Ship protect the inland shore during storms by bearing the brunt of the Gulf of Mexico's surf.

Usually. That's how it's supposed to work.

There is a National Park on Ship Island, and a tour boat makes regular round trips during the spring and summer.

Armed with summer passes, Jane-Claire and her best friend, Natalie Odessa, often travel to Ship Island for the day, and trek the boardwalk over a salt swamp to the glorious white sand and turquoise surf.

Primitive and wild, the island is a great set for Jane-Claire to film her stories about lost love, stranded lives, terrible danger, and most of all, survival.

Jane-Claire's dream of becoming a filmmaker starts here. She has a fledgling film company named White Cat Productions after Natalie's pure black cat, Bituminous.

She writes scripts that more than vaguely resemble *Lord of the Rings* because she loves heroic stories, but she is also influenced by another book she read freshman year, *Lord of the Flies*. In that story, the characters don't rise to the occasion. They lose their humanity and sink like stones.

Jane-Claire and Natalie went out to Ship Island two weekends ago. School had already started, but neither of them were settled in to sophomoredom yet.

Jane-Claire holds the freedom and immediate present of summer days as long as she can.

She took tons of footage. Sea oats waving on the dunes. Deep, clouded skies floating in the background but not enough to shade the sun's sparkle on the surf.

Her story that day was about an all-girls school shipwrecked on an island. She and Nat swam in the languid water, hot as a bathtub, and they had to keep a lookout for lemon sharks chasing smaller bait fish.

They feasted on sandwiches and drank big bottles of

sports drink. That evening, they came back to shore, happy and tanned. A Perfect Day if Jane-Claire ever lived one.

Jane-Claire leans against the back seat window of the Expedition and looks at the shoreline as her dad drives Beach Highway. The wind stirs up wavelets. Gray clouds circle in concentric bands that extend far out to sea.

When the Stevens arrive at their home on Second Street, Jane-Claire sets up her camera to take a family portrait.

She can't let their effort of dressing up in church clothes be totally in vain. Cicadas wail low and long in the August afternoon. The dark clouds make the day seem later than it really is.

Their white frame house, built on a double lot, is understated and serene. Inviting and cherished. Azaleas and confederate jasmine circle live oaks in the front yard.

Jane-Claire detects the lemon scent from the white magnolia blooms beside her mom's bedroom all the way at the back of the house. An old pine tree at the front corner of their driveway stands as sentinel.

"Do we have to? We already wasted time going to a church that wasn't even open." Lerue is not particularly cooperative. He wants to go out skimming before the police start enforcing curfew. He is a senior this year and will be off to college next, which is another reason Jane-Claire pushes to take the family picture.

"The quicker you're in place, the quicker I'll be done." She talks to Lerue as if he's a small child. He's better that way.

"Go on. Up on the steps." She uses her director's voice to arrange her family under the portico on the diminutive front porch.

She doesn't know why the photo is so important to her, but she must have known.

Jane-Claire sets her camera to allow time for her to jump in. They all smile and hug each other. She takes the picture.

THE STEVENS FAMILY PREPARES. Changed from church clothes to board shorts, Lerue is the muscle as he and Mason board forward facing windows with half inch plywood.

Jane-Claire and Dona carry a glider and the little cement goose that wears different seasonal costumes from the porch along with anything else that can be moved inside.

This is a familiar drill. Each task assigned and completed in a practiced order. The last mission is to secure the hot tub.

Mason only trusts himself to lash the brown cover to the water weighted fiberglass.

They finish. Mason and Dona go into the house and Jane-Claire looks up at the sky. The fickle wind occasionally allows a slit of blue to peek through the gray clouds.

Carrying his skimboard under his arm, Lerue bounds around the corner of the house and across the lawn.

"You headed out?" Jane-Claire squints in the harsh glare.

"I wish. The waves're kicking" Lerue stops beside his sister. "But I promised I'd wait for mom because the cops don't want anybody on the beach. Jeez." He's about to jump out of his skin, he is so excited. "Go inside. Talk to them. They're in the kitchen drinking coffee. I need to get to the beach before they close it off."

"They already did that." Jane-Claire is incredulous that her big brother thinks that she can influence their parents to do, or not do, anything. A little flattered, she decides to give it a try.

She climbs the porch steps and enters the house leaving Lerue to pace the yard.

Jane-Claire's favorite room is the study to the right of the tiny foyer. Once an outside porch, her dad and Lerue recently converted the space to what she considers her personal haven. A computer desk stands between two large windows on the outside wall. A comfortable wing chair with a reading lamp and bookshelves line the inside walls. The ceiling fan is a deep indigo blue. Jane-Claire loves it.

She sits at the desk and opens the computer. Her journal rests in its place beside a Hello Kitty mousepad. She can't possibly commit her innermost thoughts to a virtual world just yet. Handwritten on paper seems best.

Jane-Claire's journal is one of her most prized possessions. Pretty funky looking, the book is covered in denim and has a pattern of swirling colored beads all over the front cover. Kind of ugly, but she got it as a present from a friend for her birthday one year, reason enough to secure its value.

She busies herself at the computer, backs up files, but Jane-Claire mostly listens to her parents' conversation in the kitchen, a tiny, barn red, triangular space that has been updated with a pro gas cooktop, copper backsplash, and a convection oven.

There is a super-duper dishwasher and garbage disposal as well. All rooms in their house are small but everything in them is well thought out and planned. The arrangement also makes eavesdropping pretty easy.

Mason has to go in to work this afternoon, and this is the fact that the conversation revolves on. He sits at the kitchen table and watches.

Dona prepare some sandwiches to take in with him. His lab coat hangs on a wall hook near the back door.

One thing must be understood. The South is subtext and Jane-Claire's mom and dad only call each other by their first names when they are upset or down right angry.

"Mason, the storm track could shift. There's still time." Her mom talks to the sandwich. "We're boarded up. The lawn furniture's in. The hot tub's strapped down. We're as ready as we can be."

The family just got everything back in place from another hurricane warning a couple of weeks before. That storm was supposed to hit them but was a complete shoo-shoo, and instead ripped the Florida panhandle.

"Wish I didn't have to go into work." Her dad always makes the same wish, then ends up spending beaucoup time there.

Dona looks over her shoulder at him. Always the ballet dancer, her movements appear feline and fluid, one of Jane-Claire's main reasons for taking ballet herself. She likes the way it makes her feel, the strength that allows her to move as she wants. It's fun and she's good at it.

"What about disease and pestilence?" Dona cuts the sandwiches into neat rectangles and puts them into a Ziploc.

"Tell it to wait… I want you and the kids to come in with me." Jane-Claire's dad means it. He wants them to evacuate, but her mom cannot fathom a more ludicrous suggestion.

"And stay where? We don't work at the hospital. We're not part of essential personnel. Mason, we can't stop living life because you see things that don't always go right."

"I'm an emergency physician." That's dad's simple answer to most everything. Everyone dies, and he would like to prevent that as long as possible. It can ruin a person's day.

"What do you want? Wait…" Dona throws her arms up in front of her and freezes like a store mannequin. "Suspended animation!"

"Dona, I want your safety." Whoops, dad is using his doctor's voice now.

"How come you only say my name when you're upset with me?"

Although Jane-Claire doesn't see it, she hears his long-suffering sigh.

"Honey…"

Big gun time. Her mom's laugh makes Jane-Claire smile.

"Oops! Now you're really mad." Dona sashays over to dad, sets his lunch bag on the table, then sits on his lap.

"Diehard. It's against your religion to evacuate." She takes his hands and kisses him, a quick smack on the lips.

"I haven't heard mandatory evacuation orders yet… Since you have work, I don't want to go off to Gatlinburg, call it anything other than a vacation, and have you here all alone." Dona hugs him.

"When I was a girl, I remember waking up one morning with Camille ten miles from the mouth of the river. There was never any time to leave."

Dona is from New Orleans where evacuation has traditionally been assigned for northern transplants only. "Riding it out" is the term used and the preferred method for dealing with disturbances in the Gulf.

Jane-Claire formats a DVD and interrupts. She's good at that. "Dad, did you pick up the bonfire permit? What about it? I'm emailing myself all our documents and making discs of my White Cat movies. All our files are backed up. I dumped the pictures in Photobucket."

She waits a strategic second. "And mom, Lerue's waiting for you to go out to the beach with him. You don't want the police to give him a hard time, do you?"

Mason pulls Dona close and wrap his arms around her.

"Great job, J.C." Mason kisses Dona for real.

Just as Lerue enters the kitchen through the back door.

Lerue stops short, embarrassed at his bad timing. Do parents really kiss each other? He clears his throat. "Sorry… Jim Cantore's down the street at the VA. If the Weather Channel's here, we're all screwed."

Dad is still on a different planet. He looks at his son and muses. "Take my advice, Lerue. Marry your second wife first."

"Yeah…" Lerue grimaces and skirts through the kitchen. "I'll remember that… Mom, I'm ready to go to the beach whenever you are." He turns on the television in the living room.

Mason hugs Dona one more time before she stands. "Yes, J.C., I have the bonfire permit. I handed it over to mom for safekeeping." Mason looks at his wife. "Love me?"

Mom points to the lab coat hanging at the door. "Hey, I iron your lab coats."

Proof positive, but dad's request that they evacuate to the hospital and mom's decision to ride out the storm at home remains between them. Unsettled. Unresolved.

Jane-Claire's parents came from families with an operating motto of "every man for himself." That makes them both wary and fiercely independent. Every now and then when they go out to dinner as a family, the waiter asks if they want separate checks. Not today, but often enough.

Her mom is an expert in ballet, a former dancer and teacher, and her dad belongs to medicine. In spite of separate worlds, they found each other, and Jane-Claire believes they love each other, even if it means that sometimes they disagree, or don't see anything or anyone else.

Except, her dad always sees her. She admires him. His work is hard, but he makes a difference. She's taking anatomy this year for her science credit because of him. If film making doesn't work out, she might be a doc. Or be a doc first and then make films.

Jane-Claire closes the computer and reaches for her journal. She's kept the journal since fifth grade. She likes to write about what she does. What she dreams. Special days and friends. Stories she imagines that she hopes to put in a script. She writes about what matters most and she's always surprised how that changes day to day.

Jane-Claire is amazed that everyone acts so normal.

Lerue focuses on skimming, like most days, but with a tad more excitement because the beach is volatile and menacing.

Her mom gets dad ready for work, as if nothing at all is looming in the background.

Dad goes along with that, even though the church was locked, and services cancelled.

The storm gearing up in the Gulf first made an appearance on the weather channel last week. After raking the edge of Florida as a Category I, the disturbance ran straight for the heated Gulf waters. It's been growing ever since.

When Mason leaves for work, Jane-Claire follows him through the back porch and down the steps. His white coat drapes over his arm and his stethoscope hangs from his neck. She wins a bet she made with herself that he would walk straight to his prized hot tub sitting on a concrete pad behind the garage.

He snaps the straps he used to lash down the cover and checks for a tight fit. She has no idea where he expects the hot tub to go. He looks at it like the bulky rounded square might grow legs and feet and take off any moment.

Then Jane-Claire's attention turns to the dilapidated house next door. A mysterious urban legend of their neighborhood, the house holds a story that she craves to discover. She debates whether the tale is romance, tragedy, or both. Her dad thinks it's a horror story.

He's considered putting up a fence. He sent real estate agents over to ask if the occupant might be interested in selling. He went himself with a sales contract in hand. He tracked down the occupant's daughter and offered to contribute money, time, and materials to fix the place up. No deal. The owner occupant wasn't interested.

"What about Miss Adele?" Everyone knows the lady's name, but that's about it. Jane-Claire collects the rumors. Her son was a B-52 pilot. His plane was shot down in Vietnam and he is still listed as missing in action.

Miss Adele keeps deadly snakes, species that aren't even allowed into the country. She was a famous actress, and the inside of the house is a total contrast to the outside. None of the rumors are verified. She's just a name, and the house looks worse for wear every year.

Mason shakes his head and doesn't even look in the direction of the weather-beaten white structure. "I called her daughter this morning. She said she'll try to convince her to leave but... I remember that joke about a rowboat and a helicopter. God expects you to get out of harm's way if you have the chance."

Jane-Claire's not sure if her dad's talking about Miss Adele or mom.

"Does she really have pet snakes?" The house is like a magnet whenever she stands in the driveway. An Oscar winning movie just waiting to be filmed.

"Who knows? I've never been inside." Mason bends

down to rub Bituminous, the black tomcat. The cat slinks over and flips on top of Mason's shoes. He pets the cat's tummy.

"Yes, sir. You can sure smell when a hurricane's in the Gulf. Nothing but oyster shells and rot." A thin elderly man ambles up the driveway and surveys the threatening sky.

Jane-Claire likes Ed. He taught her how to catch crabs with fishing line. He has stories about an old snowball stand where he spent summer days eating the icy concoctions and counting different state license plates on the cars traveling Beach Highway.

Ed is her main source of stories about Miss Adele. He claims he went to high school with her.

Mason examines the swirling clouds. "That used to be the only warning. My great granddaddy was a bridge tender over in the bay. He stayed out one time, so he could let the fisherman in. He tied himself to the bridge pilings to keep from being swept away."

"Wash your truck today, Doc Stevens?" Ed is retired from the telephone company, but carries his bucket and sponges around on the weekends. He likes his extra spending money.

Mason pulls a twenty from his wallet and hands it to his old friend. "Not today, Ed. Catch me next time."

Ed pockets the money and reverses direction. He raises his hand, half in taking leave and half in resignation to almighty fate. "Good thing we too old to die young. God help us."

"Amen. Stay safe." Mason and Jane-Claire wave goodbye. Her dad hugs her, then turns to Miss Adele's ramshackle house.

He walks closer and shouts toward a window. "Miss Adele, don't you be so stubborn. This storm looks like it may pack a real punch. Bury the hatchet. Go stay with your family."

Jane-Claire follows at her dad's heels and takes his hand. They stand as if they're going to hear a reply any second.

She looks at her dad. "I'll talk to mom."

Mason pats her hand. "Thanks, baby." He kisses her forehead, then gets in his truck and drives off.

Fear and doubt creep through to Jane-Claire's bones. Mom may be business as usual. Lerue may think the storm is just a grand skim adventure, but dad senses gravity when it changes. No one ever expects to go the ER. No one wants to.

Jane-Claire looks after him as he drives down the street. Some houses are boarded up. Some not. It's a little past noon.

TWO

Optimistic Denial

Time crawls inside the boarded house. Jane-Claire writes in her journal, then reviews video footage of Lerue and his friends reenacting D-day. She shot the film last Sunday for his history project and is happy with the results.

Glancing into the living room, she can't miss Lerue's size fourteen feet hanging over the edge of the sofa. He watches the loop of the hurricane tracking map on the television screen with his eyes closed.

"Lerue, come see. I'm editing your D-Day landing." If he goes to sleep now, he'll keep her awake talking all night.

"Mom." Lerue hops up from the sofa to search for Dona. "I need you to come with me."

"Why?" Mom's voice booms from the laundry where she folds clothes.

"Authority, mom." Lerue makes a face. "The cops." He stands beside Jane-Claire, towering over her. "You coming with us?"

Absolutely not. Why would she do that? Jane-Claire wants to yell at Lerue and her mom. This hurricane is so ginormous that it covers the entire Gulf of Mexico, and Lerue's hell-bent on the beach.

Jane-Claire runs the footage of Lerue and his friends pulling an aluminum skiff onshore. Lerue wears their grandfather's old army jacket. Uncanny that it fits so perfectly. She fades the sounds of choppers and machine guns from the beginning of Metallica's "One" into the scene.

"Pretty good, huh?" Jane-Claire directed the filming from the top of a ladder and suggested that Lerue wear the army jacket. The guys had their paintball guns ready to go. "The perspective's better from higher up."

Lerue tousles Jane-Claire's hair. "D-day directed by J.C. Stevens and White Cat Productions. This is awesome."

Dona enters the room. "What about college applications? You promised you'd work on them this weekend."

"What about 'em?" Lerue tries to look as clueless as possible.

Jane-Claire plugs her video camera into a charger. Since the end of summer vacation, this discussion occurs on a regular, nay, on a daily basis.

Lerue stands, stumped, speechless.

His sister speeds to the rescue. "Face it, Mom. The storm's going to shut down my film editing, and Lerue's not about to get anything done on college applications tonight."

Lerue is relieved. As if on cue, a knock at the front door shelves the dispute to a distant background.

Jane-Claire gets up and moves to the door. She's been waiting.

"Natalie." She pops open the entrance, and the girls hug each other like proper friends.

At school, Jane-Claire's best friend is a pariah as much

as Jane-Claire but in a good way. Natalie is as beautiful as an exotic. Her father was blonde with gorgeous blue eyes. Her mother, Shirin looks like an African princess. And so, Nat's eyes are blue, her hair is blondish African American curl, and her lips full and expressive like her mom's.

When Jane-Claire was a freshman in high school, she was already more than a good ballet dancer. How could she help it? Dona danced in a professional company and taught ballet for many years.

Jane-Claire grew up taking her mom's classes at the studio, but Dona still warned her not to expect a decent role in Nutcracker since Jane-Claire was new on the scene and she had decided not to work at the Gulfport ballet school that year. But perfection is always a dancer's goal.

Jane-Claire nailed the part of Snow Queen in the ballet school's holiday production. Only her mom predicted the loathing hatred that flowed from the upper-classmen dancers.

The total effect was social suicide before her high school years ever started, but that is how Natalie Odessa and Jane-Claire became friends.

They were both targets.

Natalie is first chair violinist in the Admiral's Orchestra. Every Friday during the school year, she must defend her position in the orchestra to all challengers. She is a duelist, and so is Jane-Claire.

First Chair and Snow Queen teamed up. They regard school as a necessary evil, a forced mundane task that steals too much time from their real passions of dance, music, and film.

"Could you possibly come over and help me get Bituminous's carrier? My mom lost the key, and I have to go through the window in the shed. I'm afraid to go in there by myself." Natalie hems and haws the request.

Jane-Claire can tell something is wrong, and it has nothing to do with getting a cat carrier out of a shed. Nat holds her violin case close to her chest with both arms wrapped around it.

"What's up?" Jane-Claire nods at the violin.

Mom overhears Nat's request. Skeptical, she says the exact thing Jane-Claire prays she doesn't. "Sure your mom's not just looking for her stash of weed?"

Ugh. . . Mom said it.

Nat cringes and gazes down at the cork floor.

"Mom." Jane-Claire flares in defense of her friend. "I thought y'all were going to the beach." Beach comes out of her mouth, sounding a little like something else, but she stops short and tries to keep her retort clear and concise.

Nat can't be held responsible for having an unreliable mom. She just picks up pieces when she can and stays out of Miss Shirin's way when she can't. Jane-Claire wants to add that to the dialogue, but she bites her tongue, fairly unusual, not what she's known for, but sometimes in the case of Natalie, she makes a special effort.

Mom gives Jane-Claire quite the "look" as Lerue drags her to the exit.

On their way out, Jane-Claire notices that although disaster relief officials crowding the television screen demand immediate attention and Lerue pulls her by the hand, her mom rivets on the family photos sitting on top of the piano.

No one in the house plays the instrument. When Jane-Claire was young, she thought the whole purpose of the piano was to display framed photos.

Her parents' wedding portrait is prominent. Her mom soaks the picture in long and hard before she disappears through the front door with Lerue. In the photo, she and dad are very young and so in love.

Jane-Claire doesn't know that at that same moment, her dad just cleared the ambulance bay in the emergency department.

He is greeted by an all-out, all hands on deck alarm. Hospital workers carry boxes of emergency supplies. Nurses line stretchers against the walls of the emergency department hallway. Preparations plus.

Jane-Claire waits for Lerue to close the front door then turns to Natalie. "What's going on?"

"We're staying in the house, but I'm scared." Nat regularly files her nails down for fingering the violin. Today, she's bitten them down to nubbins.

"Us too. Mom's from New Orleans." Jane-Claire uses the two-word explanation for folly. "Let's go. I've always wanted to see what's in that old shed." She places her journal next to the mouse pad on the computer table and starts for the door.

Natalie hesitates, just enough and only to a degree Jane-Claire would appreciate.

"What's wrong?" She wants to add "besides everything" but Nat's obviously upset.

"I want you to keep this for me." Natalie pats her violin case and removes the strap from her shoulder. She holds the black case out to Jane-Claire.

Now, Natalie and her violin are inseparable. She practices hours a day to be an excellent violinist, not to mention stave off first chair contenders. Nat may as well have proposed giving up her hands or feet.

Jane-Claire gawks. Nothing else to do till Natalie decides to explain.

"I want you to keep it for me until all this is over." Nat's blue eyes plead.

Jane-Claire laughs, which is probably not the best

response but purely extemporaneous. "What are you going to do with your violin without its case?"

Nat grins. "My violin's in the case."

Okay, Jane-Claire's stall for time didn't work. "But Nat, I can't. Your violin is a part of you. You're the best. You can't let me keep it, even for a little while. It's got to stay with you."

"Please, and I want you to give me something of yours to protect. If we do this, I'll feel better, like everything will be alright. Like insurance. If you have it, you won't need it."

Nat's upset and not making any sense. Logic in a crisis is flawed.

"But that's not true." Jane-Claire is serious. "And what do I give you of equal value? Pointe shoes and leotards can be replaced. They have a short half-life." She rambles, but she can guess what Natalie asks. Jane-Claire glances at the beaded journal in its home base beside the mouse pad.

Holding the violin case out with two hands like a platter of hors d'oeuvres, Natalie offers it to Jane-Claire as if she's the dancer and this is the choreographed mime in Act I of a ballet.

A warning siren screams in Jane-Claire's head. Who exactly are they bargaining with?

God doesn't like stuff like this.

And the devil may bargain, but only if he's sure he's going to win. What are they doing? She feels her heart reach for her throat. The beats are loud and clear. Snatching her journal, her fingers feel the familiar beads on the fabric cover, worn in areas because she reaches for it so much. Gaudy, and of no consequence to anyone else, Jane-Claire's journal is as much a part of her as the violin is of Natalie.

Deal. The friends make the exchange. Jane-Claire

relinquishes her journal to Natalie and takes the violin into her care.

She almost sets up her camera to film the momentous moment, something neither of them can renege on, but the trade is complete.

Suddenly, they're back to discussing cat carriers.

THE SECOND STREET neighborhood survived the ravages of Camille. Mature trees line the perimeter of the street. Manicured lawns and gardens are the rule with a few exceptions like Miss Adele, who keeps the mysterious, individual, and eccentric status of the neighborhood alive and well.

Originally built as summer cottages, the homes are about fifty yards from the beach.

Natalie and Jane-Claire linger in her front yard long enough to view the swirling bands of gray clouds circling overhead.

The variable wind gusts sand and dirt airborne forming whips of trifling tornados, before abandoning the effort and moving on. The air is sticky and smells like salt. The effect is mesmerizing.

The wind practices revving up to its full potential. Potential and performance are ballet mores. As a dancer, Jane-Claire sights the goal of pushing the two ideals together to meet at the highest possible level. A prayer breaks through as Jane-Claire's fascination with the power of weather gives way to fear. No. Go away. Don't live up to the hype. Don't be as bad as the predictions.

"Y'all staying?" A man's voice startles Natalie and Jane-Claire back to earth. The Dales family strolls in front of the Stevens's house.

The two attorneys with their two little boys, a five-year-old named Michael and a three-year-old named Nick, live in a modern mansion over on Beach Highway that looks like a shoebox on stilts.

Natalie and Jane-Claire babysit the boys sometimes. They smile and wave. The boys ride their big wheels, and Jane-Claire tries to remember if she's ever seen them walking on Second Street before.

"Yes, sir. Are y'all?" She's surprised that Mr. Dales talks to them. He ignores them when they babysit. Jane-Claire glances up and down the street. No one else around.

Mr. Dales laughs. "Hell yeah, my house is built to handle anything. I used steel eye beams for the foundation."

True enough. Jane-Claire's mom complains about how awful the steel eye beams with the box on top appears each time she takes the side road past the place on her way to the grocery.

Mrs. Dales doesn't seem totally convinced by her husband's bravado. "We've taken the usual precautions." Her voice, low and hushed, is taken by the wind.

"Yes, ma'am. Only this doesn't look like the usual hurricane." Natalie throws the gauntlet down.

"Come on, boys. Let's go." Mr. Dales huffs in response and continues his walk without a glance or good-bye. Mrs. Dales's eyes implore the girls then she follows her husband and children down the street.

Stories flip through Jane-Claire's brain like pancakes. Tales of ignored warnings and parables about people eating and drinking, getting married and making plans right up until none of it pans out.

She nudges Nat in the ribs. "You just killed our babysitting job."

Jane-Claire hears the phone ringing from inside her

house. Her dad's calling for them to evacuate to the hospital and no one's home.

The girls walk across the street to Natalie's two-story house. Both of them fight not to stop dead still and study the clouds again. They stroll up the shell driveway where a leaf canopy shields them from the sky.

The shed at Natalie's house is at the very back corner of the yard. Vines cling to the outside of the worn wooden structure.

For a moment, Jane-Claire compares the shed to Miss Adele's house. Both are in a similar state of tumbledown. A purple wisteria, graceful and lovely in bygone times, gives the shed a forlorn, lonely aura, but Jane-Claire identifies some of the vines as hardy poison ivy. Leaves of three, let them be. Any Southern kid learns that, usually the hard way.

She uses a shabby rake to yank vines out of from under the only window leading into the shed. Natalie uses a smaller rake, in the same state of disrepair, to push the vines into the thick brush.

The window offers the only way into the shed. Something inside had fallen against the door to block the entrance.

Shirin Odessa, Natalie's mom, exits the back door of the two-story house to meet the girls. Her hair is a wild nest but frames her face exquisitely. If Jane-Claire were casting a movie about a lost Pharaoh's tomb, Miss Shirin would for sure be the high priestess.

Miss Shirin reaches the shed and leans against a nearby tree. She smokes a joint and spits something out of her mouth.

"Girls don't be so damn dramatic. I'm not sending you into space. It's not that big a deal. I just want you to get the carrier for that nasty tomcat."

Jane-Claire shakes her head and points to warn Miss Shirin of the poison sumac growing on the tree trunk.

Natalie hands Jane-Claire a plastic crate that she finds in the yard.

Jane-Claire turns it over and pushes it into the soft dirt at the base of the window to use as a step stool to climb up.

Natalie steadies her. Jane-Claire feels her shaking. "You don't have to come in with me."

"I'm not about to let you go in there alone." Nat doesn't want to go but nods with grim resolve.

Shirin takes a long drag and gazes up through the leaves to the gray sky. "And if you see two red Community Coffee cans. Grab them too. Okay?"

"What's in them?" Natalie's pretty ballsy to ask this of her mom. She receives a halfhearted swat from Shirin as an answer.

Jane-Claire pries the window open, and they both slip inside.

The shed bubbles with gems and junk. An old Victrola. A lamp with tattered fringe on an art deco shade. Rusted tools that could be sold to Cracker Barrel and used as nostalgic décor inside the roadside restaurant.

A doll with a porcelain face and natty hair gives Jane-Claire a start. The cold painted features stare as if to say, "Why are you intruding on my private space?"

Three-inch-long wood roaches that some people call palmetto bugs scurry across the cement floor of the shed. Jane-Claire wishes she wore her jeans and tennis shoes instead of shorts and Teva sandals. She helps Natalie down from the window.

Nat huddles behind Jane-Claire and holds onto her shoulder as if she's blind.

Jane-Claire sifts through the shed. She's not particularly concerned whether she finds the carrier or the coffee cans. She's tried to talk Nat into investigating the place for a while.

The treasure hunt is exhilarating. An old photo album holds the past close. A white French drip coffee pot reminds her of her mom's Paw-Paw. The unknown here is welcoming, unlike the unknown of the storm. In the end, she admits that both create an energy that a wild part of her desires. The pressure of danger and the promise of discovery appeal to Jane-Claire.

Natalie stays on task and spots the cat carrier. "There. Quick. Grab it. Let's get out of here."

Two red Community Coffee cans sit beside the carrier. Jane-Claire snatches them, as Natalie pulls her to the open window in full retreat.

The girls climb from the shed with a lot less fanfare than they entered with. Mission accomplished; Jane-Claire is sorry to leave.

Shirin hugs the coffee cans to her breast as the three of them walk back toward Jane-Claire's house. They're crossing the street when Lerue turns the corner at Hughes and bounds toward them. Dona is not far behind.

"Hey! Wow, you should see the beach. I've never seen the Gulf this badass. I was ramping the waves. Unbelievable. It's great, then the cops made mom call me in." Lerue wears a broad smile, complete with dimples. He gets away with so much because of that smile. He gets a bye every time.

They meet and stand in the middle of the street to talk. About a half-block east, Second Street dead-ends into the side boundary of the Veteran's Hospital where Miss Shirin works in the psych ward. The tranquil grounds and beachfront setting seem a perfect fit for recovering soldiers, just not today.

Mom talks on her cellphone. "You weren't like this when you went in. What's different?"

Jane-Claire can tell she is talking to dad. Cellphones are just coming into extensive use at the time of the storm. She's glad that he remembered to call mom on the cell.

"It's always the big one. I've heard that since I was a little girl. I remember holding mattresses against windows and cooking everything in the freezer before the electricity went out. Hurricane season comes every year." Dona fights to control her frustration, unsuccessfully.

Jane-Claire recalls a story about when her parents were first married. Her dad was an intern at Ben Taub, the huge public hospital, in Houston, and he wanted her mom to call him whenever she was going out, to the grocery, to ballet, to church, wherever. Then he wanted her to call him when she got back to their apartment. Her mom was used to having free rein of the entire city of New Orleans since she was ten. She took public transit everywhere. She returned home by herself late at night after performing in the ballet of the New Orleans Opera. Her dad's edict lasted less than a week.

Jane-Claire has a definite sense that this exchange isn't going anywhere. The Bible story of the waiting brides-maids pops into her head. They were divided into two groups, the foolish and the prepared. Jane-Claire christens a new group, the prepared stupid.

Her dad complains that he can't work if he's worried about the three of them, a common refrain and the wrong tack to take.

"Oh, so that's it." Her mom stops, brings her hand to her hip. "You don't want to have to think about us. Thanks, we're fine. We'll ride it out here. Hold on a minute…" No one ever says that to dad.

"You're doing okay, Shirin?" Mom puts her hand over

the speaker and turns to Nat's mom, who is more than amused to listen.

Shirin nods and cuddles her coffee cans. "Yip might have to see after my guys over at the VA. Depends, but I'm fine now. Call me if you decide to leave? Okay?" A cloud comes over Miss Shirin's face as if the thought of Dona not being close by makes her feel more vulnerable.

Mom raises the cellphone. "Just a minute, Mason."

Dad's voice blares. Mom pushes the phone against the front of her shirt. "You want Natalie to stay with us? If you have something at work to do, she's more than welcome…"

Nat and Jane-Claire get their hopes up, then Dona zeros in on the red Community Coffee cans. This isn't going anywhere either.

Shirin takes offense, raises her chin. "No, I take care of my own. Besides, the hurricane's not supposed to hit till daybreak."

"We'll take all the blessings we can. Let me know if your plans change." Dona holds her phone, and Jane-Claire wonders if her dad realizes he's yelling into her boobs. She motions Lerue and Jane-Claire to the cars.

Lerue waves to Miss Shirin and Natalie.

Natalie and Jane-Claire hug then separate. They wave again, and Jane-Claire moves with Lerue and her mom toward the house.

Shirin calls out to Dona one more time. "Call me if you decide to go. If you're going to leave. Okay?" Fear spikes her voice.

Shirin runs up and tugs Dona's sleeve. "You'll do that? Right?"

Dona nods to Shirin in acknowledgment, then raises the phone. "Mason, we're taking the cars to the municipal parking garage. I'll call when we get back." That's that.

She closes the call, walks to her new Ford Expedition, and gets in.

Lerue runs into the house to change out of his dripping bathing suit. Jane-Claire retrieves her video camera.

They both return in a few and pile into Lerue's older model Honda Passport. The two cars back from the house and drive down Second Street.

Natalie and Shirin wait, standing in the middle of the street, and watch them leave.

Little do they know.

THREE

Storm the Titanic

As Lerue drives down Second Street toward the center of town, Jane-Claire films preparations in the neighborhood. People place plywood over windows, pack cars, remove potential flying objects from their front porches and lawns. Everyone does what they can and hopes for the best.

Lerue rolls down both front windows of the Passport and cruises so Jane-Claire can capture the footage. She plans to film more on the walk home.

A few short blocks later, he turns into the municipal parking garage and winds up each level searching for a parking place. Nothing to be had until just before rooftop.

Dona motions Lerue into the last parking place under the protection of the roof, and she parks the Expedition on the top floor, out in the open.

Jane-Claire jumps from the Passport and runs to the side of the garage overlooking the library and the beach.

The water surge is intense. The surf crashes halfway up the beach, in some places almost to the boardwalk beside the highway.

"Everybody had the same idea. I didn't think we'd have

to park so high up." Dona talks to herself, and Jane-Claire doesn't view that as a comforting thing.

They lock the cars and start the trek home. As they walk three abreast, smack dab in the middle of Second Street, Jane-Claire is surprised, and more than a little disturbed because they don't have to move, not even once, for a car.

There are no cars. No people.

The street and houses appear totally deserted. The scene is a complete turnabout from just a short time earlier.

Jane-Claire films the desolate landscape and has no idea that she films "the before," this is how it is right now and will never be again.

Before the destruction. The looting. Before nature wipes humans aside, and so much humanity is lost by those who survive.

Even Lerue is uneasy. "Jeez, where are the zombies?"

"Orcs." Jane-Claire corrects him. "I'm looking for the big ones with white hands painted across their faces."

Mom pats her shoulder. "Our house looks empty too from the outside. With the windows boarded, you can't see lights inside, and all the cars are in the garage... Everything's okay. We'll be okay."

Jane-Claire does not believe her. She picks up the pace and jogs the rest of the way.

Lerue calls after her. "Where ya going?"

She looks back over her shoulder. "Checking on Miss Adele."

Jane-Claire doesn't know why Miss Adele suddenly surfaced and became a priority, but she believes in the importance of trying to rescue everyone on a sinking ship.

Miss Adele's house had been so lovely at one time that the peeling paint and rotten siding, the broken pieces of filigree on the front porch, and the rusted chains of her swing, are all the more sad as if the house had once been alive and beautiful then fallen into ruin.

That is exactly what happened.

Jane-Claire has never before walked up onto Miss Adele's front porch, and she's careful to avoid gaping holes in the wooden steps. The screen door is in tatters. She tries to think if she has ever seen anyone use it as an entrance or exit.

"Miss Adele. Miss Adele! You still home? It's me, Jane-Claire Stevens from next door. My dad wanted me to check on you. A storm's coming. A hurricane. You wanna come stay at our house? You're more than welcome. My mom's cooking dinner."

Clouds spin in the jaundice colored sky. The front windows rattle as they vibrate in the wind.

Jane-Claire waits, but there is no response. A tentative shuffling sound is the only reply from inside the house.

"Miss Adele." Jane-Claire rings the doorbell. Nothing. It must have broken long ago. She reaches through the torn screen and knocks on the door.

The wood, mushy and weak, feels like her hand might push through at any moment. She jumps at a slight rustle against the inside bottom of the door, but it might just be the wind.

Her mom and Lerue approach and wait at the bottom of the steps.

Dona slants the best outcome of the story. "Her daughter may have come while we were bringing the cars."

Lerue harbors no such illusions. "Come on, J.C. She's either not there, or if she is, she doesn't want you wailing at her front door. Leave her be."

He extends his arms out to Jane-Claire. She pirouettes and takes a running leap into Lerue. He catches her as if she's a small child and spins her around before placing her on the ground.

They laugh and turn away from the dilapidated eyesore.

BUT JANE-CLAIRE'S actions did have an effect on their solitary next-door neighbor, just not the one Jane-Claire wanted.

Miss Adele, a wrinkled shade of an old woman with wire tousled long hair, stood cringing at her front door as Jane-Claire knocked and called to her.

She didn't identify the storm as a threat, only Jane-Claire.

She fears the girl wants something from her or has come to do her or her pets harm.

Long after the Stevens family returns to their home, Miss Adele backs from her door and turns to her precious pets. Reptile cages stack throughout her front room.

She caresses the enclosures and coos with affection at her collection housed within, then she opens the cages and sets all of her snakes free.

STORM SHUTTERS on the windows make the inside of the Stevens's home appear dark, dingy. Jane-Claire recharges her video camera at the computer and reaches for her journal. Not there.

Nat's violin case rests against the front of the desk next to her video camera's gadget bag.

In the kitchen, Dona readies a roast for dinner. She sprinkles salt, pepper, then adds a touch of cayenne. Her cellphone rings. Mom washes her hands before she answers. She puts the phone on speaker.

"Sorry, we got the last parking places. We've been back. I just got busy." Jane-Claire wonders if her dad spots the lie. Mom just didn't want to argue with him over the phone. Too late now.

"Listen, the staff's here for the duration." Dad's voice holds a peculiar edge of panic.

"What do you mean?" Dona opens the oven door, places the roast inside. She sets the timer.

"Whoever's assigned to work the hurricane shift is locked in at the hospital until the emergency's over. Some docs evacuated with their families so relief might not be able to get back anytime soon. I might be here for several days." Mason sounds pre-tired at the prospect.

"What do you want me to do? Bring extra clothes? Food?" Dona acts dumb.

Jane-Claire touches the empty place where her journal should be, then grabs her video camera and slings the violin case across her back.

She carries them throughout the house like twins needing constant attention.

"Bring you and the kids. Get over here. Pack clothes. Bring air mattresses." Mason's voice is sharp, impatient. He's used to being obeyed without question.

Jane-Claire films the study then drifts to the living room where Lerue sprawls on the sofa. He waves at the camera, makes the universal sign for "they're coo-coo" by spinning his pointer finger around his temple, then points toward the kitchen. She shoots paintings on the wall, photos on the piano, china displayed in corner cabinets.

"No, we're settled in." Her mom's tone is final. But Jane-Claire disagrees. They should drop everything and go. Just leave. Now. No questions asked.

She flies into the kitchen, efficiently opening cabinets and filming the contents.

"The hospital locks down at five. I've made arrange-ments. Staff relations has a room for you and the kids. I have passes for the cafeteria." Dad explains as if that might help persuade mom to listen.

Dona smiles, waves at Jane-Claire running camera, then turns deadly serious again. "You're bribing me with hospital food? This neighborhood made it through Camille with no water in any of the houses. No significant damage."

Cat 5 Camille remains the gold standard, the bench-mark. Records are made to be broken.

That's when Jane-Claire tries to take over. She pauses her camera and grabs the phone. "Hey, Dad. We're on our way." She looks at Mom. "We can't stay here. What time is it? We have to go. Dad's waiting for us."

Jane-Claire has the same effect on her mom as she did on Miss Adele.

Dona glares at her. Her resolve to stay in the house rather than evacuate to the hospital galvanizes. She chases Jane-Claire around the kitchen, trying to retrieve the phone.

"Move it. Five is cut off." Mason sounds relieved and cheers J.C. on.

Jane-Claire holds the camera in front of her as a shield and the cellphone high over her head. She runs from the kitchen into the living room and backs straight into Lerue.

He plucks the phone from her hand and gives it back to Dona, who is more than a little angry.

Dona talks into the phone. "It's four forty-five. We're staying put. We don't even have cars. Remember. We can't get there in time."

Vanquished, Jane-Claire forgot that one little detail. Her mom is right. There's no way they can make it to the hospital before it locks down.

"Pace yourself. It's going to be a long night. We're prepared." Dona throws a kiss into the phone.

For what? A sprint or a marathon? Jane-Claire wonders.

Natural disasters can occur in a flash or at least in a relatively short time span. Tornadoes run rampant then peter out. Mudslides move through then dissipate. Hurricanes last for hours on end.

"I'll bring you fresh clothes when I can. I love you." Dona snaps the cellphone closed and puts the phone in her pocket. "Lerue!" She yells his name way too loud.

Jane-Claire stands in front of her mom, waiting for her to pass sentence on crimes of interrupting and interfering. She is guilty but doesn't believe for a second that she should've kept her mouth shut. She just wishes that she had persuaded her mom to leave sooner.

Lerue enters the kitchen and stands beside Jane-Claire. He looks sleepy, relaxed as if the storm has come and gone, and he has just come in from a good day skimming.

Dona straightens. "Lerue, you vac. Jane-Claire, dust. I'll get the bathrooms."

This is sheer idiocy. Jane-Claire gives it one last ditch attempt. "Mom, we don't have time for that. Maybe we can still get to the hospital. Maybe if we run or if we're late, we can beg to be let in. Just say that we're Dr. Stevens's family. They'll make an exception for dad."

"Why do we have to clean?" Lerue moves past evacuating to the task at hand.

Which gives Dona the perfect opportunity to ignore Jane-Claire's plea and spout a classic line that brooks no opposition.

"Because I say so." That's it. The end. They are not going to evacuate. They are going to stay, and possibly go down with the ship, but the house will be clean. Jane-Claire can't believe her ears.

Lerue makes a face but obeys. He threads his way through the tiny hall of a kitchen and grabs the vacuum from a pantry closet.

"You've got to be kidding, right?" Jane-Claire stares.

Dona hands her paper towels and glass cleaner.

Jane-Claire struggles to hold all the cleaning supplies Dona piles on top of her, plus the violin case and her camera.

"I'm not about to have a dirty house. Do it." Then Dona adds a qualifier. "Pack two days of clothes and your school stuff in your backpacks. Just in case."

For a fraction of a sec, Jane-Claire thinks her mom changed her mind.

Her mom pulls her cellphone from her pocket and looks at the clock, but then she pushes the phone back into her jeans. "What kind of homework do you have?"

Jane-Claire's face falls. All evidence says they're done for, yet her mom maintains that everything will be fine. That is the superpower of denial.

Lerue answers Dona from the living room, yelling above the din of the vacuum cleaner. "Not much. School will be out at least till Wednesday and J.C. has my D-day project ready."

"Here at the end of all things... Our fellowship is formed." The quote is appropriate, and Jane-Claire may never have a chance to use it again.

Dona smirks, irritated and doubtful at the same time. "I see Natalie gave you her violin."

"To protect and defend." Jane-Claire pulls up. As a ballet dancer, she plays the drama game well. "Yes, ma'am, and I won't leave it behind on a march to Mordor."

"How about saying some real prayers?" Dona pulls a cleaning caddy from under the sink.

Mom has no idea. Jane-Claire's praying like crazy. Danger is coming. She's consumed by that uncomfortable tension, and the feeling that she's entombed. She wants to go. Leave. Don't stop for anything. But instead, she helps her family clean the house.

After she dusts, Jane-Claire films the contents of her room. Her white iron bed with brass knobs stands in the far corner. A framed *Lord of the Rings* poster dominates the wall. A life-size cutout of Legolas guards the door. She reviews the details she so carefully constructed.

A lot of the things in her room she has had since she was little. American Girl dolls. Random photo albums.

She wishes she could go over to Natalie's house. She wonders what her friend's doing, whether she found Bituminous and if she was able to corral him in the pet carrier. He would be sure not to like that. She remembers Sunday afternoons and playing ping pong on the back porch or volleyball in the yard. She wants everything to stay just as it is, as much as her mom.

As she packs the last of her textbooks and school supplies, she questions why her mom is worried about their homework. Her backpack is so stuffed that there is no room for the few personal belongings she wants to bring. She prays for her dad waiting for them at the hospital.

MASON PACES in front of the ambulance bay doors, half expecting to see Dona and the kids walk through the entrance. All is quiet and ready as it can be in a hospital.

Differences in barometric pressure between interior of the emergency room and the storm outside cause the wind to trigger the automatic doors to open. Air rushes into the room, along with trash that spirals through the doors and speeds down the hall.

Mason shields his eyes from the dust particles.

Lori Sandt, a young nurse, has had her eye on Mason for a long time. She's been careful to be helpful, respectful, and open to any suggestions.

"This is making me so nervous. Why do we only have three patients?" She smiles at him, inappropriate and only meant for the beholder.

"Curfew. Nobody wants to chance going out right now. Police are still patrolling. Don't worry. It'll be interesting soon enough." Mason is matter-of-fact and doesn't really notice Lori.

"That storm is headed straight for us." Lori nestles close to Mason.

"Just wait it out." He steps away, closer to the doors, and searches the ambulance drive. "Sometimes, storms veer right before they make landfall. Computer models have been known to be wrong before."

The automatic doors almost close, then the swirling wind and the pressure difference forces them open again. Lori cringes against Mason. "Isn't there any way to stop that?"

"Nope. We take all comers in the ER." He stands like a rock and keeps vigil on the driveway.

Mason's mindset tends to be reactive because of his job. He waits until problems are brought bleeding and injured before him, then he acts. He's conditioned that way, and that is the main difference between him and Dona. She is proactive, always looking for the best strategy and tactics for a situation. Mason waits. That's what he's good at. Waiting and dealing with whatever is thrown at him.

"Is your family here?" Lori steps between Mason and the automatic door.

Mason shakes his head and looks around her. "Yours?"

Tears form in Lori's Bambi eyes. "My ex took the kids to his mom's in Hattiesburg. I'm afraid I'll never see them again."

"Come on. You have custody, right?" Mason places his hand on Lori's shoulder.

This time, Lori looks out as litter streams past the ambulance entrance. "After this, who's going to be around to enforce it?"

Suddenly, Mason admits the problem brought before him and laid at his door. The storm is one event, but aftermath is another. It may be possible to survive one, but only through sheer luck or the grace of God will anyone make it through both.

INCREASING ALL EVENING, gusts of wind hammer the Stevens's house. Candles stand ready on the coffee table.

Jane-Claire settles next to Lerue on the sofa and watches FEMA officials drone on about the coming doom. Lerue is already asleep. Her sweet, trusting brother, who has such awful confidence looks like a young child, but he helps calm Jane-Claire's nerves.

Unlike her mom, who flutters around like a carpenter bee caught in a trap. She gathers books, places them in boxes at the foot of the attic ladder, which is pulled down and extended in the small hallway that connects all of their bedrooms and the bath between. She snatches photos from the piano and starts another box.

Then the Governor's wife appears on the television. The older whitish haired woman wears no makeup and a raincoat as she stands in the makeshift studio. She's exhausted and she doesn't sugar coat a thing. Apolitical, she talks as if she's your mom or best teacher.

She says, "You should evacuate." Not if, but you should. "If you have not yet evacuated just. . . Get out. Get out. Get out." She says it three times.

Jane-Claire looks to her mom, who stands beside the sofa staring at the television. "Why didn't they say that earlier?"

Jane-Claire wants to remind her that they did, but she didn't listen. The time for evacuation is done. The storm is upon them. About to make landfall.

A shuddering wind blast startles them both. The electricity goes out. Pitch dark.

Jane-Claire freezes in place. Her mom whispers in the thick black. "This is so stupid." She can only agree.

Dona pulls a flashlight clipped to her jeans and lights the candles on the coffee table. Her cellphone protrudes in her pocket. Jane-Claire grasps the opportunity.

"When can I get a cellphone? They really come in handy." Her smile appears a little ghoulish in the shaky dim shadows.

"Put on your Tevas," Dona advises.

Okay, so that didn't work. Jane-Claire nudges Lerue and hands him the river sandals. Their backpacks lay on the floor beside the sofa. Jane-Claire straps the velcro on her Tevas first, then hooks Lerue's for him. He moves slowly, still asleep.

"Bike gloves, goggles, and a helmet. Dad packed them." Dona shoves two nylon gear bags into her hands. Jane-Claire can see her regret at not leaving the house, concern and worry are all over her face.

Of course, he would. Jane-Claire's dad often says that he never saves anyone, only that he delays their death.

How can he smile, which he usually does, after witnessing so much tragedy? Life is complicated and contradictory.

Lerue hugs his nylon emergency bag and drifts back to sleep. Jane-Claire, clutching Nat's violin case and the gadget bag holding her video camera, wonders if Natalie and Miss Shirin are at their house or the veteran's hospital.

Dona goes to the front door. She opens it just a tad, only to peek out. The force of the wind almost bowls her over. Howling as if it's heard a good joke, the wind causes the wood door to creak and strain.

Jane-Claire cowers into the sofa.

Dona musters all her strength to close the door and keep it from flying open. She walks through the living room. Like a guardian angel, she keeps watch over her charges. Her shadow flickers larger than life on the walls. Finally, she pivots the recliner next to the sofa, away from the dark television, to face the boarded living room window. She stretches out in the recliner and the shadows still. Dona and Jane-Claire both fall asleep as bands of rain and sheers of wind pound the house.

FOUR

Worst Fears Delivered

Slow moving time often speeds to a crash. Like when a person waits. . . for anything. Or on a pristine spring day. Maybe think of an afternoon, when you're walking on the beach or playing in the waves. Time seems frozen, then in a flash, it's over.

Lerue and Jane-Claire sleep like puppies on the sofa. Their legs tangle, and they hold their dad's emergency packs like old stuffed rabbits. Dona curls on the recliner.

First light breaks around the edges of the plywood covering the windows and shines in Jane-Claire's eyes.

A bleak, gray, glaring light that drowns the yellow butter glow of the candles burning on the coffee table. The relentless wind is at full tilt. Limbs and debris hit the outside of the house, but she feels safe. They made it through the night after all. Why not?

Because at daybreak, the most intense part of the hurricane moves onshore.

The worst is yet to come, and the terror begins with an ear-splitting crack, followed by a brittle snap. A massive something hits the front of the house followed by the din of splintering plywood and shattering glass.

Jane-Claire doesn't know what is happening but the pine tree at the front corner of their lot topples diagonally, sheering off the portico above the front porch and taking out the plywood and the front bay window.

She gasps, but her tiny cry drowns as the wind enters the house, like a dragon seeking prey.

Lerue springs from the sofa. "What the... Get up. Quick!" He drags Jane-Claire from the couch and shields her from the glass fragments and wood fragments flying through the living room.

The straps of the nylon emergency bag hook around her arm, the thin bands bite into her flesh.

"Mom." Lerue yells as he pulls Jane-Claire into the small hallway and to the attic stairs.

Jane-Claire reaches for her video camera, and barely catches the strap of the violin case. She has a fleeting image of her journal being lost forever.

Dona jerks awake, as if she just dreamed she had fallen off a cliff. She pushes against the floor, and the recliner flips backward.

The base of the recliner saves her from being sliced by shards of glass catapulting into the house. "Go! Go! The window's blown!"

She grabs the backpacks and her own gear bag, raising them to protect her face from the projectiles.

Irregular shards hang from the windowpane. The television screen cracks and the doors of the television cabinet rip and break into pieces, riddled with glass. The furniture tumbles in the gale.

Jane-Claire struggles to open the gear bags and don the protective goggles and gloves. She pulls her helmet on and straps it down under her chin. Dad was right. They need every bit of his emergency cache.

She squints even with the goggles on because the air fills with particles. She bunches her T-shirt up over my mouth and nostrils because she can't breathe dirt.

Lerue and Dona pull their gear in place as if they are going to war. The bizarre scene plays in the tiny hallway that connects the living room, bath, and bedrooms.

The wind howls and upends every treasure in the place. Paintings, books, a vase of flowers. So fragile. So easily destroyed.

A weird fascination takes hold of Jane-Claire. She wants to film, to record the event. She steps outside of herself to become an observer of a force that overcomes everything in its path, but the danger is present tense. This is no time to document.

Lerue climbs the attic stairs. Dona passes the backpacks up to him. He reaches for the violin case and Jane-Claire's video camera, but she shakes her head. Those items stay with her. Dona lifts a box of her books, then a sound like a roaring freight train pierces the air.

Jane-Claire covers her ears with her hands.

Dona pushes her into the small bathroom and shouts to Lerue. "Get down. Tornado!"

Mom and Jane-Claire stand in the tub and hold onto each other.

"Lerue. Lerue!" Jane-Claire screams her brother's name, but the wind sucks her voice away.

Lerue jumps down from the attic stairs, then bursts through the bathroom door, hauling the double mattress from his bedroom.

Stepping into the bathtub with them, he wedges the pad into the opening using it as a protective barrier. The small bathroom window is not boarded with plywood, and daylight illuminates the bathtub shelter. Blood oozes from cuts on Dona and Lerue's faces and arms.

Jane-Claire doesn't see any glass in them, but that doesn't mean it's not there. She notices the smallest details with precision and focus. She looks down at what she wears and is horrified.

What is she doing in such a God awful atrocious looking outfit? Forest green plaid flannel pajama pants that she bought from the fundraiser for Lerue's swim team, her gray Dutch Mafia T-shirt, and Teva river sandals. Her hair, dirty and tangled now, is down, and she wears her glasses under the goggles.

Her mom told them they needed long pants the night before, but it was hot out, so she didn't put jeans on like Lerue. She just grabbed what she wanted to sleep in, and that happened to be baggy, too big pajama pants, the only other long pants she had handy. Big Mistake.

The tornado rampages from the beach.

The sound nears. Trees fall, and houses twist apart. An old Victorian, much larger than their own home, stands on the lot next to them. A young couple lives there with a little baby boy. The husband is an airline pilot, and one of the best people you'd ever want to meet. He always has a smile and a wave. She prays that they evacuated.

Through the unboarded bathroom window, Jane-Claire sees the tornado split the Victorian apart and carry it away. Nothing left. Siding, shingles, and boards rise and travel at the storm's whim. Her prayers translate to screams for help.

Jane-Claire looks away, unable to take in the images anymore. An envelope protrudes from her mom's hoodie pocket. She snatches it.

"Don't lose our bonfire permit," she scolds as if she is so angry at the possibility.

Dona and Lerue bust out laughing.

"No, sire!! Can't lose that!! Yeehaw!!" Lerue yelps and whoops as if he's at the annual rodeo down at the coliseum.

Jane-Claire laughs with them as long as she can. She's so nervous that she could run on air if need be. Some people cry. Some people get angry. Some people just hide in a corner, but she laughs. She looks at Lerue and Mom. It must be a family thing, because they all laugh long and loud, at least until the tornado passes by.

Then she hears the water.

At first, only a trickle then a continuous running sound like someone turned on a faucet full blast and walked away.

AT THE HOSPITAL, Mason dances with chaos and triage runs like a war zone, but he still gazes over to the ambulance bay doors every chance he gets.

The electricity in the hospital is out.

Years earlier, after Camille, the hospital put in diesel emergency generators and dug several artesian wells. People thought the administrative board was overreacting, spending money they didn't have but when Mason grabs a chart, at least he can read it. All courtesy of the emergency lighting.

A triage nurse approaches him from the opposite end of the hall. "X-ray's overheated. Lab's malfunctioning. EMS units can't get out. The ambulances are too boxy to drive in the wind." She's breathless by the time she finishes.

Mason listens and remains calm. "Thank God we're as prepared as we are."

"We're the only hospital still open." The triage nurse, mouth slightly open, pants for air.

Stunned, Mason rejects what he just learned. Perspiration drips from his face. "What about Biloxi? Garden Park?"

The triage nurse shakes her head. "All flooded. We're the only hospital open in a ninety-mile radius."

The ambulance bay doors swoosh open. Two high school age boys struggle as they carry an elderly woman on a house door used as a stretcher.

The woman is disoriented, hysterical. She screams, moans in pain. Her hands grab at invisible objects in the air. Her eyes see what just happened, not what is happening now.

"Her house flooded. Ours did... too." One of the boys tries to explain to Mason. The boy's mouth opens, but no new words escape.

"Her husband had her piggyback. He was going through the debris and lost his footing. He threw her out of the front door." The second teenager's eyes are glassy, wide.

"The house collapsed. It crushed him. Ben saved me, and the house crushed him." The woman jars to the present and belts out a wail that brings shivers to all who hear it.

Mason gets to work, but his face contorts to control the heavy emotion. He glances one last time at the ambulance doors and the fury outside, then points to an empty gurney.

"Put her over there." He looks at the Triage Nurse and adds, "The bus just pulled up."

STORM SURGE GUSHES INTO THE STEVENS' home. Water fills the structure so fast and sure that soon it is deep enough for the intense wind to create waves. Debris floats into the house with the waves.

Water rising on the outside of the empty, dry bathtub that Jane-Claire, Dona, and Lerue stand in is an astonishing sight that happens too fast for anyone to laugh.

Jane-Claire lifts the violin case with her video camera in its gadget bag and balances both on top of her helmet. Despite latches and zippers, the carriers are water repellent not waterproof.

"Quick! Move to the attic!" Lerue shouts. He leads the way, clearing a path by using the mattress like a bulldozer to push aside the thick coating of debris.

Jane-Claire steps from the bathtub into the dank knee-high water and sloshes to the attic ladder in the small hallway. They hold onto doorframes and walls to keep from being drawn down into the under tow.

Dona looks into the rooms of her home, her bedroom, the living and dining rooms. Furniture, paintings, lamps, her carefully packed book collection, buoy up in the water or are smashed by the wind into walls like battering rams.

The television cabinet reaches critical speed and takes out the wall between the living room and her bedroom, including the framing studs and water-logged sheetrock. The material breaks apart and bobs away in pieces.

"Don't look. Go. Just go!" Lerue pushes his mom along. Stopping is dangerous. He battles to shove the waterlogged mattress into the living room.

A viper snake slithers on top of one of the waves.

"Move it! Go!" Lerue's startled gasp demands attention. The urgency in his voice unmistakable.

Jane-Claire clambers up the attic stairs. Lerue shoves Dona ahead of him, then follows her into the attic.

The attic, floored with plywood, has a high pitch and is crammed with Christmas boxes and old toys. The area is dry and safe, for now. Safe becomes a relative term to Jane-Claire during the hurricane and remains so to this day. She doesn't believe that any place will ever truly feel safe again.

She sits on a box marked "Lerue's Dinosaurs" and gazes into the glaring gray-white light filtering through chinks in the roof.

Her brother was such a big dinosaur fan that he used to walk around the house like a raptor, stalking and curling his arms beneath him, as if he had talons for fingernails. Details from their childhood drift through her mind. Small things.

Lerue sits on a box marked "Christmas Decorations."

Mom sits on the edge of the attic entrance, absorbed by the destruction. She breathes through her mouth. Her eyes full of fear and shock. She forces herself to pull away and look at her children.

"Is anyone hurt?" She pulls her legs beneath her and stands to inspect their faces and arms. She dabs at the blood on their clothes, faces, and arms with her shirttail.

Lerue does not like to be pawed at, and true to form, he has a lot of trouble sitting still. He yanks his bike helmet off and throws it to the attic floor.

"Why does dad give us this crap?" He yells to an unseen audience.

Jane-Claire looks at her mom. Dona looks at Jane-Claire.

The answer seems pretty self-evident, sort of like the Constitution. Welcome to the disconnect zone. Explaining dad has always been like trying to elucidate a cosmic mystery. For a moment, the storm takes second place, lurking in the background.

MASON IS at a flat-out run between patients on the

stretchers and wheelchairs jamming the halls of the emergency department.

"Code Red. Room three twelve. Code Red." Even the voice on the public address system sounds edgy with panic.

The announcement brings him to a full stop.

"That's so random. I've never heard of a Code Red. What is it anyway?" He asks his question to no one in particular, but Lori touches his shoulder as if she's been waiting for an opportunity to explain.

"South-facing windows are being blown out. Over fifty so far. Upstairs, they're moving patients into the halls." Her hand lingers on his shoulder until the last possible moment then they hurry on their separate ways.

JANE-CLAIRE HAS no intention of feeding Lerue's beast, so she refuses to engage him directly but decides that she has to do something to break the monotonous strain.

She opens a box marked "Nativity" and removes the painted plastic figurines that grace the front lawn at Christmas. A camel, donkey, and shepherd are first to appear. Then the three wise men plus Mary and Joseph fill the small space of the floored attic.

Jane-Claire doesn't realize that she's creating an impromptu church, and with it, a calm and peace. Last from the box is a little crib and the baby Jesus. He smiles at her.

Lerue may be irritated, but at least he's quiet. Bingo. She knew this would do the trick.

"What are you doing?" He glowers, peeved but not enough to buck the whole nativity.

Jane-Claire shrugs. "I have my video camera. I'm setting a scene." But really, she's praying for courage. That's the best.

Mom follows her lead and places Mary near the crib and infant. Even Lerue joins in to set the Wise Men in the panorama. Jane-Claire gets her camera out and films.

Lerue has a heart to heart with Joseph. Dona places a reassuring hand on Mary's shoulder. The scene plays out with a backdrop of rising water and jumbled floating trash visible through the attic door opening.

Later, much later, they can hardly look at the footage because their faces are so open. Fear. Resolve. Repentance. Faith. Their emotions are so visible and laid bare as if their eyes were able to see that day in a way that is not possible during "normal" time.

Lerue's stomach growls. "I'm so hungry." He turns to Mom who, of course, is the wizard from which all food appears.

"Seriously?" Dona sighs, then the corners of her mouth turn up. "I have leftovers in the fridge."

Lerue doesn't think she's funny.

"Don't you have anything? I'm starving." He wraps his arms around his stomach and leans forward, rocking back and forth.

"I was going to feed this to the seagulls at the beach yesterday afternoon." Dona digs in the lower reaches of her hoodie pocket and pulls out stale biscuits from White Cap wrapped in a paper napkin.

Lerue grabs the biscuits and portions them into three shares. Dona shakes her head, refuses to eat. No wonder all the moms on the Mayflower died in Plymouth during the first winter. They gave all their food to hungry boys.

Jane-Claire is not as gracious. She grabs a piece of biscuit and takes a bite. "Lembas bread tastes pretty good."

"Hunger's the best seasoning." Dona has said this to her children for years, but as the day grinds on, they come to understand what it means. Time drags in the heated humidity, and they wait, forced to shelter in place as disaster officials say.

Jane-Claire listens to the wind and worries about what is happening on the other side of the roof. The noise is so loud that maybe she doesn't want to know, but the quiet in the attic is somehow worse.

They all sit, folded in on themselves in a vertical fetal position. Dona's eyes are closed, but she's not asleep. The tension in her body is too visible. Lerue looks anywhere, everywhere like a cornered animal.

Jane-Claire clears her throat, a small paltry sound but Dona and Lerue look straight at her, riveted.

"Hurricanes should have southern names like mine. You know, double ones." She wants to break that inside silence so badly.

"Like Billie Jo?" Dona smiles.

Jane-Claire nods. "Yeah. There's Mary Mac, Sarah Beth, Judy Faye."

Dona studies the strained rafters and runs through the names of her former ballet students. ""Savannah Grace. Madison Lynn. Emily Ann."

"How 'bout Bubba Yaga?" Lerue chimes in. They laugh. "That'd be one heck of a storm if it lived up to that name."

When Mason was in kindergarten, he had to travel to school from his house way out on the Auburn Opelika highway. Bubba Yaga was a bully and their dad's arch-nemesis on the dreaded school bus ride.

They laugh again but more subdued. All the sweet southern names whisper away in the sound of waves echoing through the house.

Racing inland, the circular storm shifts wind direction. The house creaks and groans in powerful blasts. One violent gust takes down a limb that punctures the roof at the back of the attic. A partial breach.

Dona and Jane-Claire scream.

Lerue jumps to his feet and bashes his head on a rafter.

"Agh." He staggers. Lerue will have a shiner of a black eye for weeks to come.

"I bet that hurt." Dona helps him sit down on the box. She looks around as if other limbs are on the attack then hands Lerue his bike helmet.

He rubs his head and pulls the hardhat on, fastening it in place. That's why dad put the helmet in his emergency bag. Mom doesn't say a thing. Lerue hears her loud and clear.

Gradually, the wind subsides and although still unsettling, it sounds more like someone shrieking the next block over.

Jane-Claire peeks through the attic opening into the flooded house.

Lerue huddles over, still rubbing his head and more unnerved by the quelling sound than the former intensity. "Why is it different all of a sudden?"

"The eye passed us now." Dona nods. "So, the wind's blowing in the opposite direction."

Dona and Lerue join Jane-Claire at the attic opening. They all peer down into the house.

The storm surge recedes almost as quickly as it first swamped the living room.

Layers of mud and sand, along with tons of debris are left behind. Furniture, and what seems like all the refrigerators within a mile radius, litter the interior along with tree limbs, countless unidentified detritus.

All Jane-Claire can think is that she helped clean the house not twenty-four hours earlier. The thought makes her giddy, then depressed.

"Everyone's stuff floated through the front window." Lerue shines a flashlight into the rubble, searching for the viper.

The neighbors across the street had been selling off the contents of their home all summer. They bought an RV, a beautiful Tiffin motor home, and planned to tour the country living like nomads. Their original airstream trailer was one of the only items they had left to sell, and it is now lodged through the bay window and sticking halfway into the Stevens's living room.

Dona notices light streaming through the hole in the roof. "Let's try to get out."

Lerue doesn't have to be asked twice. He beats Dona and Jane-Claire to the opening. Squeezing and contorting his body around the limb and busted roof timbers, Lerue pushes himself out of the attic.

"Hey, Lerue. Help me." Dona reaches for the opening. She raises her hand to Lerue. He stands on the roof, shading his eyes from the glare. He doesn't seem to see Dona. He turns in a slow circle before stopping to face the beach.

"Lerue, help me out this minute." Mom's voice commands him this time.

Lerue looks down through the escape hatch. "I'm not sure you want to see this."

FIVE

Wiped Out

Jane-Claire is last to make it out of the attic and onto the roof. She holds her video camera and has the violin case and gadget bag strapped to her back.

She doesn't know what she expected. She heard the wind and saw the storm surge, butJane-Claire is totally unprepared for the landscape before her.

Color, along with any distinguishable landmarks, are erased. The trees, what is left of them, look like scrap wood.

She stands with her mom and Lerue on the apex of the roof and confronts Armageddon.

Here is the apocalypse.

How can they deal with doomsday?

Jane-Claire does not cry. Her eyes are dry. They sting and itch. An almost out-of-body shock response takes hold. She can't process all that has happened. Too weird.

She stands in a sea of what was people's lives and is now an ocean of junk. Holy crap. How did this happen? Insane. She's never seen anything like this before.

Her thoughts race. Where can they go? What are they

going to do? What about school? Yesterday, she was working on a history paper due next week. Everyday life vanishes.

Now, Jane-Claire questions if she can get off the roof and walk anywhere without getting a nail or glass in her foot. She can't react to this normally, because nothing is normal.

The house is still standing.

At first, she reflects that's a good thing, but then must admit that it's only a shape of a house. Maybe her family made out luckier than the neighbors whose homes vanished, but does that mean they're better off? The house is there, but what benefit is it? The structure is not livable anymore.

Jane-Claire's video camera hangs useless at her side. Her mouth droops open. She faces the hurricane fence that lived up to its name, at the back of their property.

The chain-link barrier leans very slightly in the direction of the railroad track bed rising a short distance behind it. The mound of broken everything piled against the fence is staggering.

Sound is swallowed up. No calls from birds or insects, only the ominous hiss of broken gas lines. The smell of natural gas spewing into the air is overpowering.

Debris surrounds their house and fills the backyard. Her dad's precious hot tub lodges on its side between two denuded tree trunks.

Jane-Claire raises her camera and shoots the video. She usually does an introduction, but what expression should she have on her face? Smile and say, "Hi, we're here" or just stand there with some mix of severe and silly?

Whatever she does, the film will be a timestamp that can never be changed. The camera weighs on her, so heavy that she can hardly lift it to her eye.

She presses the record button, then turns in a circle, and zooms in on particulars. The roof of their garage/guest apartment rests directly on the ground. Every supporting structure underneath is washed away.

The airline pilot's Victorian disappeared. Nothing on the lot but stacks of boards and broken furniture. All of their neighbors' homes are either gutted shells or gone altogether. Concrete slabs and exposed footings are the only evidence that houses ever stood on the scrubbed lots.

Refrigerators lay busted open everywhere. Pelicans act like vultures and gobble up whatever food they can find in the open fridges. Jane-Claire spots Bit, Nat's black cat, fighting with a pelican for a piece of fried chicken.

Clothes and treasured linens from closets dry perpendicular in the broken limbs of oak trees. The salt laden cloth flies like stiff flags from the branches.

"Oh, my God." Dona gasps for breath. Ever notice that these are the first words that spring to mind when horror finds you.

Lerue slings his backpack over his shoulder and forges out into a debris field so vast that he can easily step from the roof where they stand onto boards overlaying the top of the rubbish.

"Lerue, wait," Jane-Claire panics. She yells after him.

But Lerue skims along on the top of the boards, way ahead.

Jane-Claire turns the camera off and thrusts it back in her gadget bag. She adjusts her backpack in front of her and the violin case and gadget bag on her back.

"What does he think he's doing?" Mom mutters under her breath.

Lerue stops and looks back. "Get to the railroad tracks, then we can walk to the hospital. Come on." He jumps over boards and climbs over trees like a giant blonde monkey.

"Lerue, hold up. Wait for us." Mom shouts at him then looks to Jane-Claire. Skeptical and cautious, they start out on the unsteady wreckage.

"I'm almost there." Lerue's voice sounds distant over the damage sea.

Her mom is afraid. Every man for himself. Jane-Claire squeezes her hand. They try to match Lerue's pace, but reckless abandon isn't their style. The wobbly fragments are full of broken glass and protruding nails. Lerue didn't look for the danger, but they see it all. Jane-Claire takes point and moves as fast as she can.

"Slow down, Missy." Mom hasn't called Jane-Claire Missy since she was ten. She freezes in place but balancing on the shaky stacks is as hard as climbing over them. Think *Lord of the Rings* and the disintegrating bridge in the Mines of Moriah.

"Keep moving. If we fall, we'll be hurt." Great advice. Theoretically, but the pure desperation of their situation suddenly crystalizes. They are so not ready for this.

"These gas lines could blow in the heat," Mom's voice shakes.

"No. Everything's soaked." Jane-Claire doesn't know when she became the expert, but she moves on. She wants to get to her dad. More than safety. More than obedience.

"Agh." A rickety board trips Jane-Claire. She falters and tries to clamp her mouth shut, but that's beyond her control. She's in freefall. Every bit of her will and concentration focuses on continuing to walk.

"I've got you. Now, just slow down," Dona says as she springs forward and catches Jane-Claire's hand. "Take it as easy as we can."

Jane-Claire catches a parting glimpse of her home's

dark windows and torn siding. The tree limb that appeared so enormous when they were in the attic looks no bigger than a twig, compared with other limbs and tree trunks lying helter-skelter around the house.

Bituminous walks the roof's ridgepole as if he doesn't have a care.

"Bit... Bit." Jane-Claire calls to the cat that wouldn't think of coming to her on a good day.

"Natalie. Natalie..." She calls in the eerie quiet for her friend. "Mom, I can't see Natalie's house." She hunts for landmarks, but all that's visible is a clear, unobstructed view of a trashed beach.

"It's not there." Dona puts her arm around Jane-Claire's shoulders and turns her back in the direction of the railroad tracks.

"Where is she? We have to find her." Jane-Claire jerks away, but her mom seizes her arm with a strength that she doesn't expect.

"No. What would Dad say? He'll be mad as a hornet as it is."

"But mom... What if..." Jane-Claire stops. She can't say any more. She feels the tug of her friend as if Nat has taken hold of her other arm.

Jane-Claire is pulled in two directions.

"We're not certain they stayed at the house. Shirin would have taken her to the VA. She wouldn't leave Natalie alone. We'll send help as we find it."

"We thought... We exchanged what we valued most. My journal. Her violin. . .. What about Miss Adele?" The eyesore house of their neighborhood is absent. Jane-Claire doesn't see any filigree and all the wood is broken.

Dona softens her grip but turns her daughter away. She continues to hold Jane-Claire's hand as they forge a path and pick their way over the rubble.

Jane-Claire looks down into a web of debris. Silver trays, toys, kitchen tiles, a broken piece of a carved cornstalk bedpost.

Suddenly, she spots something else and halts. Jane-Claire gasps.

A pair of small pink tennis shoes with the owner's feet still inside lies beneath the rubble. The little girl's legs are ashen, scraped, and still. No blood left. No life.

"Tell me next time you're going to stop." Dona sways, dizzy with shock.

Jane-Claire points through the web tangle.

Dona sees the little girl's body and sobs.

"God in heaven." Her hand flies to her mouth, and she shields J.C. as best she can. She hugs her daughter, then grabs her chin and meets her eyes. "Jane-Claire, you listen to me. It's my fault we stayed. Remember this poor child. Be grateful we made it through this storm."

"I want to go home. I just want to go back. I want to go home." Jane-Claire borders on hysteria. She lurches from her mom's grip.

Jane-Claire leaps to snatch a fluorescent orange bicycle flag on a long white pole from the ruins. She sticks it as a marker in the spot where the child's body lies.

"Be grateful we have our lives." Dona pulls her along.

That's not always easy to do. The orange fluorescent bike flag waves in the hot breeze off the Gulf.

Lerue paces back and forth along the track bed, waiting for the slowpokes.

In back of their home, railroad tracks sit on top of a raised rail bed that acts as a natural levee. Lerue helps Dona climb onto the solid ground. Jane-Claire scrambles after her.

The inland side of the railbed is literally the "other" side of the tracks with modest to low income homes. Old shot-guns and shacks with incredible oak trees in the yard crowd the tiny lots. There is some damage. Trees and power lines are down, but the homes are relatively unscathed. People sit on porches. Children frolic on the fallen tree limbs.

"Ed's house made it. His neighborhood looks pretty good." Lerue points to a worn shack that looks little better than Miss Adele's and laughs. "He lived on the right side of the tracks."

"All the expensive homes are on the Gulf side. What irony is that?" Dona shakes her head as if she might cry, but she regroups and walks on.

Jane-Claire hikes between her mom and Lerue. They pass Hughes Road, the cut-through from the beach inland, and traverse over more debris.

An older man sits on the other side by the track bed. He stares into the devastation, tears in his eyes.

Raising bottled water to Dona, he does not even look at her. He pulls two additional drinks from a cooler beside him for Lerue and Jane-Claire.

"Sir, thank you for your kindness." Dona tries to talk to him.

Never has bottled water from a superstore tasted so amazing, but the older man does not turn. He is consumed by the scene in front of him.

Two National Guardsmen walk in the distance.

"Wait a minute," Jane-Claire leaves her mom and Lerue and runs to the soldiers. She points to the bike flag, barely visible in the distance.

The Guardsmen take off in the direction of the little girl's body.

Jane-Claire looks across the remains of their neighbor-hood to the beach as she waits for her family to catch up.

Four steel eye beams, poking out of the sand, are all that is left of one house's foundation.

"Is that the Dales house?" Jane-Claire pulls on Lerue's T-shirt.

At the same time, Lerue yells and runs to a young boy sitting on the edge of the railroad tracks. He reaches Michael Dales and scoops him up in his arms.

Dona and Jane-Claire sprint after Lerue.

"Hey buddy, how's it going? Where's your mom and dad? Where's Nick?"

Michael buries his face into Lerue's chest and points to the four pieces of steel.

"I'm taking him with us." Lerue's voice leaves no room for argument.

Dona nods and continues down the railroad track, her head down, and shoulders rounded. Jane-Claire hugs her and prays that dad is glad to see them.

People buzz all over the place, news crews and the first round of looters armed with plastic grocery bags and grabbing anything they can find.

The two National Guardsmen are the only authority in sight.

No residual rain clouds linger from the hurricane. The sun is bright and red hot in a cloudless sky. The tempest did its worst and moved on, leaving nothing but destruction.

Jane-Claire pats the violin case on her back. At least, she won't disappoint. Natalie's treasure is safe.

At Memorial Hospital, they stand in line to get in the ambulance entrance. That's the debut of the expression, "Things can always be worse." This phrase is repeated over and over in the next months, and Jane-Claire ponders what it really means.

Being grateful for surviving, she understands. But often

people say the phrase to discount or belittle a person's experience, loss, or pain. Things can always be worse, but sometimes she wants to scream, "Things can always be better" right back in the face of someone who just said this to her. If her house burned to the ground in a house fire, it would be counted as a terrible tragedy.

Jane-Claire's heart aches to see Michael cling to Lerue. The sheer volume of patients in the emergency department is frightening. The faces of hospital personnel as they hurry among them hold a resolute panic, and dad is nowhere in sight.

"Excuse me, I'm Dr. Stevens' wife. Do you know where I can find him?" Dona is polite, sincere as she catches Lori Sandt's arm.

Jane-Claire knows Mrs. Sandt's son, who is in her sophomore class at school. He's a sullen boy with hair, home dyed orange, and multiple piercings. He's a pain in the ass, but he writes well. She reads his stuff.

The woman recoils when Dona identifies herself as dad's wife. Mrs. Sandt likes dad. Jane-Claire can tell by the way she treats her mom.

"He's busy. Maybe he's in the cardiac room." The woman spits the words and walks on.

Dona threads her way down the hall. Lerue carrying Michael, and Jane-Claire follow like ducks.

At the cardiac exam room, they step to the side and try to keep out of everyone's way as they wait.

Jane-Claire wants to see him, but then she doesn't because he'll be angry, especially with mom. She just can't predict how much.

Mason bursts from the exam room.

Dona charges toward him. "Mason, I'm sorry to disturb you."

He doesn't stop, doesn't even slow down. Mason writes an order in a chart as he continues down the hall.

His family trails after him.

"Mason, we have Michael, the Dales's oldest son. He needs attention." Dona starts with something neutral.

"Sign him in at the desk." Her dad is as angry as Jane-Claire has ever seen him.

"We walked from the house." Dona jogs to keep up with him.

"Where else?" Mason's retort is as predictable.

Lerue, flashing a telling sideways glance, says he's worried, tired, anxious, devastated, and above all, hungry.

Jane-Claire runs up to Mason. "Dad, our house is the only one left on our side of the street."

"I'm up to my ass in alligators. I can't stop because you finally decided to show up." But Mason doesn't stop. He exchanges charts with a nurse, not Mrs. Sandt, in front of an exam room and quickly scans the new information.

"Look at us. We made it." Jane-Claire waves her arms in front of his face.

"Dad, furniture's piled to the ceiling inside the house." Lerue steps closer to Mason. Michael whimpers and hides his face against Lerue's shoulder. "Refrigerators, pieces of a Hobie Cat sailboat, a red surfboard. I want to keep it if we can't find the owner. Kathy's airstream is sticking out of the living room window."

"Not everyone made it." Jane-Claire whispers the comment, doubting that her dad would hear.

Data that has nothing to do with vital signs doesn't mean much to Mason.

Until Lerue adds one final detail. "The hot tub's upended between two tree trunks."

"Shit." Mason winces and looks straight at Lerue. That hurt but it did get his attention.

Mason actually looks at them all.

Dona, Lerue, and Jane-Claire appear pretty stupid looking standing in front of him wearing bicycle helmets and gloves, goggles dangling from their necks. Blood from cuts and scratches spots their clothes. Bruises are starting to show. Lerue has a heck of a black shiner. Between his lid and cheekbone, his eye is almost swollen shut.

"You all need tetanus shots," Mason says, with a straight face.

Older Nurse sides next to Mason. "You have a fine family, Dr. Stevens. Just say you're glad to see them."

"I am but…" Mason looks down, then reaches out and gathers his family in his arms. He hugs them briefly then separates.

Dona shrinks. "But" is a word that negates all words preceding it. Have fun but. . . Glad to see you but. . . I love you but. . .

"You could've all been killed." Mason turns on Dona.

"I'm sorry, Mason." Dona can't hold back her tears. "This is a disaster."

"My point exactly." Mason grinds the words between his teeth.

"Mason, I'm sorry." Dona waits for a sign of forgiveness from him. Nothing. "Gulfport's destroyed. We lost everything."

"Not everything." Mason touches her arm. Enough for now.

"Dad, what're we going to do?" Jane-Claire is not quite sure what she expects him to say, but she demands he say something.

Mason kisses her forehead. "Endure, J.C. Endure."

Mason pushes into the next exam room and leaves his family in the crowded hall.

They stand, blocking the passage for a moment, then Dona turns to Lerue. "Let's go check Michael in."

Older nurse pats Dona's arm. "Honey, you're hurt. Blood's all over the back of your shirt. Come with me."

Jane-Claire didn't even notice her mom's shirt, torn and soaked with blood. She didn't see it before that moment. Pinpoint adrenaline focuses instinct. She only saw what was necessary for her own survival.

SIX

Before and After

The large atrium at the front entrance of the hospital is usually filled with plants, a few chairs, and sunlight, but today, it is crammed with patients and supplies.

Lerue stays behind with Michael in the emergency department, so Dona carrie the backpacks and Jane-Claire the gadget and violin case.

They weave their way through patients lying on gurneys and mats in the atrium, trying not to step on anyone.

"Are you okay, Mom?" Concerned, Jane-Claire asks. Her mom acts like she's on autopilot and hasn't said much since dad went on with his rounds.

"Yeah, I'm superficial compared to all this." Dona skims the area with nervous, flighty eyes.

"Do you think Michael will be okay?" Jane-Claire can't believe she says this, but the question is out of her mouth before she can swallow it back.

How okay can he be? How can any of them ever be okay again? She bites the inside of her cheeks to keep quiet.

"As much as possible. There's a protocol. The hospital will contact next of kin. We don't know if he was separated from his family or. . . Let's pray they're all okay and just got split up somehow." Dona scans the scene again. "This looks like a *Gone with The Wind* reenactment."

"Good one, Mom. *Gone with the Wind.*" Jane-Claire actually laughs, although the sound is raspy and hoarse.

She pictures the scene with Scarlet running in that balloon of a dress through the wounded lying everywhere. What a terrible scene. Not funny at all.

Dona forges a path to the checkpoint table manned by two overweight security guards armed with Glocks. They are no nonsense and have grabbed the inflated power of gatekeepers.

"Driver's license." The first security guard eyes Dona as if she's a criminal.

She fishes through her wallet and hands the guard her license.

"I just got mine last week." Jane-Claire gets her paper learner's permit out. Her summer Driver's Ed class seems like a long time ago in another life. She's nervous and running her mouth overtime. "I'm proud to have it."

"Congratulations." The second security guard cracks a dull smile.

Dona clears her throat. She doesn't believe disaster is an excuse to be rude.

"I have wristbands for you." The first security guard places a plasticized paper wristband on Dona.

She rubs her wrist as if the band burns her skin.

Upstairs on the fourth floor of the behemoth building, the emergency lighted hallway is deserted. Dona and Jane-Claire walk carefully down the hall because the tile floor is wet and slippery with condensation since the air conditioning is off.

They pass a public rest room where maintenance men manually empty waste from a toilet.

"Nasty." Jane-Claire chokes on the organic smell.

"Those men are brave and steadfast for cleaning it." Dona focuses on not falling. "So many conveniences of modern life just stop without electricity."

Jane-Claire takes her mom's hand. They ice skate over the glazed floor to Room 317, an interior room labeled, "Echocardiography."

Dona checks the room number and title of the room against a slip of paper the guards gave her then swings the door open.

Inside, the room is pitch dark. Emergency lighting from the hall barely penetrates and air in the room is thick with chilled humidity.

Two gurneys draped with white sheets are pushed into a far corner and medical equipment, a blood pressure cuff and otoscope, hangs from the wall.

"It's freezing in here." Dona shudders as she stands beside her. They shed the backpacks, gadget bag, and violin case, and hug each other because that's the only real right now.

Dona pulls her cellphone from her pocket and turns on the flashlight.

Two human bodies lie on the gurneys in the corner.

A floor nurse rushes into the room. "Oh, I'm so sorry. We haven't been able to take them down to the morgue yet. No elevators. We thought you weren't going to use the room. It's so nice and cold in here."

Dona nods. "I understand." After today, she can understand just about anything.

LATE THAT EVENING, the Stevens family sits together in the

hospital cafeteria. The large room is packed but eerily silent, as if the people are only ghosts and only going through the motions. Plates and silverware move but don't make a sound.

They eat only because they have to. The food has no taste.

Jane-Claire is not sure what it is, an approximation of meat, runny mashed potatoes, and greens of some kind. She's never seen anything like it before.

Even Lerue can't stomach it, but her dad has somehow managed to eat the whole thing.

Jane-Claire sits across from her dad and next to her mom. Lerue sits beside Mason. They never sit in a pattern like this at home. Jane-Claire wonders why.

Mason makes the first move. "You're telling me that there's nothing you can salvage."

"You didn't see it, Dad. We'd need chain saws and heavy equipment." Jane-Claire wants to scream at him. She clamps her mouth shut.

"I guess we could try but I don't really see how." Dona hasn't touched a thing on her plate. "You have to believe the unbelievable, Mason."

"But if that's true…" Mason deliberates out loud, without realizing that he's just stepped into an open manhole.

"What? You think I'm making this up. You're hearing stories in the room." Dona flares. "I was there. I've never seen destruction on this scale before."

Mason switches his empty plate for Dona's full one. He smashes some meat into the mashed potatoes and shovels a bite into his mouth.

Dona is horrified.

He looks up, meets her eyes. "Then take the kids and leave."

Mason stuns his family.

Lerue half-stands and hits the table with his hand. "Dad, you need my help. You can't do this alone."

"You do as I say." Mason slaps him down. "You're telling me that this whole area is a dead zone. If that's really how it is, then it will be that way for some time to come. No food. No water. Dona, I want you to take the kids and go to Kit and Martin's."

"Alabama?" Dona's mouth straightens to a thin line as if Mason just asked her to evacuate to the moon. "No. I don't want to go off without you. That's why I didn't leave the city to begin with. No."

"Not quite... Don't rewrite history." Mason doesn't miss a beat. He smiles rather mean and raises his hands. "You wouldn't leave the house. You refused to listen to me. You put our children at risk and did what you wanted to do instead."

"How was I to know?" Dona droops.

"Because I came to work and saw the level of prep. I knew, and you didn't listen." Mason growls at his wife.

"I said I'm sorry, Mason. Please. Can you just let it go?" Good posture is Dona's natural state but today she's bending under the weight.

"Most of the docs are gone. We're down to two surgeons. There's no one to take my place. I'm telling you to take the kids and go." Mason makes a fist and almost hits the table. Almost.

"Honey, you're asking me to go backwards. The kids may have been born there, but it's been years since we lived in Huntsville."

"Kit and you are old friends. You were roommates. You went to college together. We were neighbors."

"Not intentionally." Dona pouts.

"Martin's a good guy. I know they'll help." Mason acts so sure.

Jane-Claire and Lerue observe their parents along with anyone sitting close enough. They listen to their hushed whispers. Hear the panic and dread lining their voices.

Lerue leans forward and puts his hand on his dad's shoulder. "Dad, you need me to rebuild the house."

Mason shrugs him off, but Lerue tries again and holds on harder the second time. "And I want to be here for Michael. I want to check on him. He hasn't said anything, and no one's been able to find his parents or grandparents. Please. Let me stay with you."

Dona interrupts, "You have to work on college and scholarship applications. That's a fact that hasn't changed at all."

Lerue's temper rears. "That doesn't mean anything now. School will be out of commission for months."

"It means your future. You're a senior and you get one chance."

Mason turns to Lerue. "Son, we're not to rebuilding yet. We'll reassess but right now, I need you to go with mom and your sister, so I can work."

"I get it." Dona pushes her plate away. "We're just a distraction."

Dona and Mason whisper, but they might as well be screaming at each other. They hiss and sigh, scared like children struggling to find their way in the dark. They seem so young but maybe Jane-Claire confuses indecision with sadness and straight out fear.

Mason takes Dona's hand. His voice is soft, even loving.

"We can't make a right decision now. Everything's too fresh. Too raw. I say Huntsville. Are you going to fight me on this? Again?"

Jane-Claire shakes her head. Everything might have been fine if he didn't add "Again."

Dona yanks her hand away and stands. Her chair scrapes against the floor, that awful fingernails on the chalkboard sound.

Everyone in the dead silent cafeteria looks up and stares.

"I don't have a choice." Dona throws her napkin on the table and walks from the room.

THE LAST TIME Jane-Claire slept was on a sofa in a home which doesn't exist anymore. She finds it really hard to sleep with a single blanket on the cold floor of a room that was used as a temporary morgue a few hours before, but she manages because she is so tired.

She wishes she would sleep and never wake up.

Then the door to the echocardiography room opens. Her dad closes it behind him to keep the emergency lights in the hall out and fumbles through pitch dark over to the gurney. He trips on Lerue who only grumbles, turns over, and promptly crashes out again.

Jane-Claire opens her eyes as wide as she can, and she can't see a thing.

Her dad reaches the stretcher and shakes mom's shoulder.

Dona sputters awake. "What's going on? Are you okay?" Stock questions to buy the time it takes to really wake up. She slides from the gurney and hugs at Mason who crawls onto the thin plastic covered mattress and curls into a fetal position.

She takes his shoes off. "Mason? Talk to me. What's happening?"

"It's unbearable down there." His voice sounds thick

and far away. "I had to be careful not to drip sweat into wounds when I was sewing. Emergency lights aren't bright enough. I had to get a nurse to hold a flashlight, so I could see to sew."

"Keep talking. Let it out." Dona smooths her husband's hair.

Jane-Claire wonders how two people can be so at odds then take care of each other so well, as if the cafeteria conniption never happened.

"The lawyer family on Beach Highway. . ." Mason continues.

"The Dales. Michael's parents." Dona brightens, "Did they come in? Is everything okay?"

"No. Far from it." His voice is flat. "They all drowned. The younger brother too. The kid's grandparents came and got him but they're in their nineties. God help them."

Jane-Claire covers her mouth with her hand and fight tears. All hopes of happy endings up in smoke.

"Lerue would take him in a second." Dona fishes, begs the question. "Maybe we could. . ."

"That boy is all those old people have left. Would you take him from them?"

"No." Dona's answer sounds like a breath.

Her mom would take him, and Jane-Claire wants her dad to say that he would too, but he moves on. "And Miss Marijuana. . . That crazy psych nurse who lives catty corner."

Jane-Claire listens hard. Nat. . . . Where's Nat?

"She brought Natalie in with a broken arm. Got caught in something when they were swept from their house. Angulated fracture. She might need surgery."

"No." Dona is as upset as Jane-Claire.

Jane-Claire presses the violin case to her chest. It doesn't matter which arm. Nat needs both of them.

"You should've listened to me. It could've been Jane-Claire or Lerue." Dad won't give it a rest.

Dear God. Jane-Claire would rather it be her that got hurt than Nat.

Dona swallows her tears and her anger. She climbs onto the gurney and hugs Mason.

Jane-Claire lies still and waits. She doesn't have to wait long. Their breathing pattern soon changes. She gets up, lifts the violin case, and sneaks from the room.

HOSPITALS ARE SUPER SCARY PLACES, but especially at night when the electricity is out. Jane-Claire creeps down the halls, a little less slippery than when she first came up to the echocardiography room, but now the floors are streaked with dirt and sand.

The elevators aren't working so she listens for activity in the stairwell and runs down the stairs as fast as she can when she doesn't hear anything.

She tightrope walks the red line taped on the floor to the hall leading to the emergency department, but she may as well have just walked in the direction of the noise.

The ER sounds like a party is going on, just not a party Jane-Claire wants to go to. Children scream. People cry and sob. One man yells the F word every time he opens his mouth. What the emergency department really sounds like is hell.

Jane-Claire has no idea how she's going to find Natalie. If Nat was taken to surgery, then this is a completely wasted trip, but she has to try. The violin case hangs from her shoulder, the deep indented mark from the strap may be permanent.

Then she pictures Natalie's joy when she will be reunited with her violin. It doesn't even matter to Jane-

Claire about the journal as long as Natalie is happy about the violin.

Serious and determined as she walks down the hall, Jane-Claire soon appreciates that she doesn't need to bother worrying that anyone will see or stop her. It's easy to blend in with chaos.

She scans faces as she walks. Not a single one has she ever seen before. A dismembered hand floats in an orange Gatorade bucket, the big one that football players pour over coaches' heads after they win a game even if it's cold outside. Dirty sheets stained red with blood and brown with. . .

The stench is overwhelming. The emergency department smells like a sewer and Jane-Claire wishes she was wearing her contacts to keep the odor from making her eyes water.

Old Nurse suddenly cops her from behind. "What are you doing here? Your Daddy's upstairs. I told him to go myself not thirty minutes ago."

Jane-Claire jumps and spins around. Old Nurse is the perfect person to help. Jane-Claire takes her hands and gives Old Nurse her best imploring look. "I'm trying to find my friend. She broke her arm."

Old Nurse points her in the direction of a linen closet. She tells Jane-Claire that it was the last clean place and warns her that Natalie was too upset to stay in the hall.

JANE-CLAIRE ENTERS the linen closet like a conquering hero returning with spoils, then stops short. The shelves are empty. The emergency lightening casts angular rough shadows through the tiny space. What a downer.

Natalie lies on four armless office chairs that have been pushed together to act as a makeshift bed.

Jane-Claire is first repulsed by the idea, then remembers her blanket on the cold floor. Four chairs pushed together sounds like a great idea, and she makes a mental note to look for some when she gets back to the fourth floor.

Memaw, Natalie's elderly grandmother and Miss Shirin's mom, squats on the floor next to her friend. She hums a low and mournful tune. She's never liked Jane-Claire because she's white, but that's okay, Jane-Claire says she understands. Not really. She's afraid of Memaw.

The old woman's head snaps up and she snarls, "What you want, girl?"

"Hey, it's me. Jane-Claire. Natalie's friend. I have her violin. I kept it safe for her during the storm." Jane-Claire holds the violin out toward Natalie. A round of applause might be nice.

"She don't need that thing now." Memaw raises her hand as if she's warding Jane-Claire off.

Natalie stirs on her bed of chairs and starts to cry. "Bit was in the carrier."

Jane-Claire is not entirely sure what she means for a minute, then she remembers seeing the black cat sunning on the ridgepole of the roof after fighting the pelican for a fried chicken lunch.

She kneels beside Natalie. Memaw only tolerates her proximity.

"No, Bit's fine. He got out. I saw him this morning." My God. Jane-Claire is taken back. Was that this morning?

"You're just saying that." Natalie cranks up the sobs. "Bit's dead."

When Natalie spots the violin case, she really lets loose. "I can't play my violin. My arm. It hurts. I can't." Nat tries to talk between sobs. Unsuccessfully. She wails and writhes on the bed.

Memaw and Jane-Claire work to keep the chairs from coming apart. Nat's really not going to like it if she gets dumped on the floor.

Getting Natalie upset was the last thing Jane-Claire intended. She thought she'd be deliriously happy.

The whereabouts of her journal pops into her thoughts, but she banishes that little selfish gremlin.

"Please don't cry. I saw Bit. He's fine." Jane-Claire considers, then abandons the thought of going back for her video camera. "Maybe you can't play right now, but you need your violin. You'll play again, and I kept it safe for you."

What did she want? A medal? A gold star? Lerue is brilliant, so brilliant that he calculates the exact grade he needs to get to make an A in a subject. He never makes the highest grade by sheer design. He keeps his academic achievements on the quiet side.

Jane-Claire is like her dad. She goes for the extra credit. She doesn't just want a perfect score. She wants a hundred and ten percent. She likes to own it. She plans for extra credit, but she admits that Lerue has far more friends. She has Natalie. One friend.

Lerue tells her that she always wants to be the teacher's pet and that this is her fatal flaw. Jane-Claire yells at her brother when he says that to her. Then he lowers his voice and says that she'll just have to find out the hard way.

Jane-Claire guesses that she just did. She places the violin on the floor next to her inconsolable only friend who rants about a cat.

"I was trying to get him out of the house. I just wanted him to be safe. How can I play a violin? I'm first chair. How can I defend my position now? What am I going to do?"

Isn't that the big question?

Jane-Claire scrunches closer to Natalie. "Nat don't beat yourself up. You'll get better. It'll be a long time before school gets going again. You have time to heal. You'll be okay."

She spews all this stuff, and Jane-Claire wants to believe it, but is not sure she does. She never thought she'd see Nat, who is so sweet and good, get dealt such a blow.

Memaw shoos Jane-Claire away as if she's the cause of all this. Then she grasps that Memaw is right. She's the person who stirred Natalie to a frenzy.

The old woman snorts. "Your daddy's a doctor. Your family'll land on its feet."

"Where are you going with this?" Annoying old hag. Jane-Claire stands and faces the woman. "We lost everything."

"Rich get richer." Memaw doesn't look anything like Miss Shirin or Natalie. She's coal black with big white eyes.

"I think we should all help each other the best we can." Jane-Claire was one to talk. She thought this was a great idea. All she did was heap more pain on disaster.

"I can't play. It's all I had." Natalie turns her back on Jane-Claire, faces the chairs and cries, "It was my hope. My dream. All gone. It's over."

If Jane-Claire had been alone with Natalie, she might have kicked her and told her to get a grip, but she's afraid Memaw might kill her if she tries the tough love approach. She goes for logic.

"Natalie, you need your violin and I have it for you. You gave it to me to protect, and I did. Please stop crying." Her words don't touch at all.

Natalie can't even hear them over her sobs, and Jane-Claire is bothered because she sounds like her mom.

Memaw pulls at the T-shirt of her God awful outfit.

Jane-Claire startles. "What'd you give her? What'd she keep?"

Jane-Claire is mad this time. "I gave her my journal. I've had it since fifth grade."

The old woman gives her the stink eye. Jane-Claire is ashamed, like her end of the swap wasn't good enough.

"My journal means a lot to me." Jane-Claire sounds like a child having a tantrum. "Nat, I'll keep your violin safe. Until you want it again. I'm upstairs if you need me."

"Upstairs." Memaw hoots, amused and angry at the same time. "And we stuck here in this hot little linen closet."

"At least they don't park dead bodies in here." Jane-Claire backs from the room. "I'm sorry, Nat. I'm so sorry I disturbed you."

Jane-Claire takes the violin and rushes out of the room. Her face is hot. Her body's dirty and sticky.

Hurrying down the halls, she almost falls more than once. She runs back up the empty staircases, takes two steps at a time. She thought she'd feel lighter on the way back, but she lugs the cumbersome violin case, weighted with a burden she may never get rid of. Her friend may be gone.

Jane-Claire's journal is important to her. She wrote in it over seasons and years, but there is something she holds more dear.

SEVEN

Exodus

Mason stands with his family outside the ambulance exit. Another hot, humid day. FEMA arrived during the night, and the hospital personnel are pumped to get some help, but Jane-Claire takes one look. Deep dread.

Busy beavers erect circular white modular tents complete with generators and air conditioning, but there's an obvious problem which is overlooked.

Jane-Claire notices right off, and so does her dad. They glance at each other, the only communication they need. Sometimes when people try to help, they don't think of the people they are helping. They just help themselves.

The white circular tents effectively block the transfer of patients to and from the ambulances. The EMS can't pull up to the wide double doors to off load.

Two emergency medical technicians struggle to push a gurney carrying an injured patient around the tents and up the sidewalk from the parking lot to the entrance.

"What dumbasses!" Jane-Claire mentally screams and shakes her head.

Her dad reaches out to hug her. "Try to call when you

get there." Mason looks at Dona. "This is the best thing right now." Saying that doesn't mean it's true. "Just be careful getting out of here."

"Mason, I'm not even sure if we still have cars." Dona's irritation surfaces.

"You parked on the top floor of the garage. Let's hope for the best." He spouts platitudes and clichés galore.

But Jane-Claire can't speak any words to replace them. Maybe that's why they're used so often.

Three FEMA physicians stand in a closed circle, wearing coordinated fresh starched uniforms with personal water canteens strapped on their back. They only notice each other.

"Hey!" Mason wearing wrinkled scrubs looks like a homeless person next to them, but that doesn't stop him. He walks up anyway and gestures to the EMT's manhandling the stretcher up the incline of the sidewalk. "How about lending a hand?"

Mason can be compelling when he smiles. Jane-Claire guesses that's where Lerue got his charm from.

The FEMA physicians break rank and join with him to get the stretcher into the emergency department, but they don't move the tents.

Dona nudges Lerue and Jane-Claire. Time to go. All the plans they thought were their life are gone. They see one step ahead. Beyond that is blank.

Jane-Claire waves to her dad. Dona and Lerue are already walking in the opposite direction.

Mason doesn't even know that they are gone. He's at work now.

AS THEY TRUDGE to the municipal parking garage, Jane-Claire has an idea of where they need to go, but questions how they're going to get there. They need to find a school. Lerue must go to college. They have to keep on going. and that is when Jane-Claire links their journey with the quest of the fellowship in *Lord of the Rings*.

She is super into the trilogy. Jane-Claire's film ambitions first sparked after seeing *Return of the King*, released in December two years before.

She loves looking at all the different characters and imagining storylines. She got her video camera that Christmas. She never thought she would be filming this.

When they arrive at the garage and even after all they had already been through, all the strange, terrible sights they witnessed yesterday, they are still not prepared for the scene in front of them.

Cars parked on the lower levels of the garage look like they played bumper boats and floated together with no care about the parking lanes.

Dinged and crumpled vehicles pile against each other, like toys in a careless child's shoebox. One car looks as if it climbed up on the cement railing and is ready to jump off.

Tangled trash and debris weave the wire fences that separate the different garage levels and she is surprised that despite the jumbled mix, there is still appears to be an opening wide enough to drive out of the chaos.

Dona and Lerue forge a path up the ramp. Jane-Claire lags behind. No one is in a real hurry. She walks to the edge of the garage, the side facing the beach.

Waste, tree limbs, and twisted metal litter the white sand. Fallen from a cargo ship docked at the port, metal containers lie split open on the beach, with bags of dead chickens spilling out of them.

A sea breeze kicks up and Jane-Claire recoils from a strong whiff of rotten decay.

She gags and stuffs her T-shirt against her nose and

mouth. The rotten chicken carcasses smell toxic, absolutely lethal.

Shielding her nostrils, she looks down at the remains of the library. The roof and front wall of the building are missing.

Looters swarm over the stacks within and steal wet books from toppled shelves.

Why? She doesn't understand. The books are ruined. They'll probably never even read them.

Lerue puts his arm around Jane-Claire and leads her away from the edge. They climb together up the final two floors of the garage. The sun blazes.

Lerue shades his eyes and rubs his forehead. His Honda Passport, parked on the inland side of the garage just under the roof, is dinged and dirty, but overall looks okay.

Dona's Expedition is parked on the rooftop.

Dona calls a full halt when she meets her SUV. The Ford Expedition is almost new. Mason and Dona compared models and debated long and hard before deciding to make the purchase.

All the windows, front, back, and side are broken. Nuggets of tempered safety glass surround the parking place. The side directional mirrors hang next to the front doors, useless and attached only by the wires used for remote control. The paint on the SUV is so scraped that the color appears as steel gray.

"Holy shit." Lerue says what they are all thinking.

"Is that our car?" Jane-Claire asks the question, hoping she's wrong.

Dona lifts her remote and presses the keyless entry. The mangled Expedition beeps back.

. . .

JANE-CLAIRE RIDES shotgun with Lerue in the Passport. Dona leads the way in the Expedition which to their surprise actually starts the first time she tries.

She squeezes the car between the misaligned cars on the way down the ramp, using the wrecked Expedition once or twice as a battering ram to get out of the garage.

Getting out of town sounds like a simple thing to do because there's no traffic on the road, but debris covers the streets. They must drive over boards, cracked lopsided concrete, and debris that they can't identify.

Jane-Claire prays they don't get a flat tire.

The grocery stores and pharmacies near Beach Highway are completely destroyed. Nothing is left but the steel frame and tons of rubble.

It takes them over an hour to reach Highway 49, which is the road to the Interstate and out of town.

As they drive farther inland, they see a couple of pharmacies are open. People stand in mega lines that go from inside the store to circle around the outside of the pharmacy building.

People wander aimlessly, as if they see nothing in front of them, but neither Lerue nor Jane-Claire have the heart to call them zombies.

Fallen trees crisscross the roadway. Traffic lights aren't working, and directional signs are absent, blown away or crumpled.

Lerue follows Dona who drives on what she thinks is the right road. Interstate-10 is closed to all traffic, so they continue north on what they guess is Highway 49.

Southern Mississippi is a mass of pine trees, so there are not many landmarks to judge distance or direction. All they know is that they drive north, away from the coast, slow-going.

Water and wind damage extend inland for miles and

miles. All the canals, bayous, and streams that had any outlet to the Gulf overflowed their banks by the hurricane's wind and storm surge. A lot more than limbs are on the road.

Dona dodges entire toppled trees blocking the road. A couple of times, they're unable to even drive on the road. Lerue follows Dona as she off roads onto the shoulder or median boundary to avoid obstacles.

They travel all morning and are not even to Hattiesburg, only about 50 miles north. The day drags on. They drive for hours, picking their way over and around detritus while trying to stay on the road.

Jane-Claire glances at the gas gauge of Lerue's Passport. She hasn't been able to take her eyes off of it for miles now.

"I know. E means empty." Lerue winces but keeps driving. "I see it but there's no place to stop. Nothing's open."

"I think we're almost to Hattiesburg." Jane-Claire does her best to sound hopeful. What she's really hoping is that mom in the Expedition ahead is keeping a lookout for them in case they run out of gas.

A long line of retreating cars blocks an intersection that travels west. Lerue stops in the traffic.

"Should we turn the engine off?" Jane-Claire questions if they're even on the right road. "Which do you think is better? Keeping it on while you stop or turning it off?"

Lerue flipped off the air conditioning miles back. He winces and groans behind the wheel.

"What's the matter?" Jane-Claire says a prayer that they don't run out of gas.

"I don't know," Lerue breaths the words out. "We have to keep going."

Jane-Claire doesn't know what he means, just that he's not making great sense.

The debate whether they should turn the engine off or leave it running becomes a moot point when mom darts onto the left shoulder and passes the cars in line to continue down the road.

Lerue follows her, and almost slides into a shallow ravine.

"Watch it! What are you doing?" Jane-Claire gasps.

"Staying up with mom." Lerue breathes slowly, as if he's hurting.

Jane-Claire turned the radio off a long time before because the only station they could tune into was from New Orleans. Rising water overtopped the levee near the 18th Street Canal and other levees are breeched and broken.

"The city is flooding. The city is flooding." The announcer kept repeating the line over and over.

Panic acts like a sugar high. Shaky and weak, Jane-Claire wonders if Lerue feels the same way.

"Do you think it's true? About New Orleans?" She talks nonstop to Lerue, who is pale and sweating. "The whole city? How can that be? Do you feel okay? What's wrong?"

Lerue looks as if he's going to be sick.

Then Jane-Claire sees Dona's blinker signal. A rural gas station in the distance looks like it may be open.

She points to the Expedition. "Take it easy. Pull off behind mom. Easy."

"Migraine." Lerue whispers the words, then barely manages to steer the Honda off the road.

He kicks up gravel and dirt as he pulls up next to the Expedition at one of the pumps of the old '60s style station. He kills the engine.

Dona's Expedition sputters and grinds to a halt, which is pretty sad. Brand-new, now ruined.

Two good old boys gee haw out in front of the station. They look up when the two SUVs pull up.

Lerue stretches both arms out over the steering wheel. He leans over his arms and groans.

Jane-Claire exits the Passport and rushes to Dona.

"Lerue's feeling sick. He says he has a migraine. And we're almost of gas." Jane-Claire couldn't quite bring herself to say completely out of gas. She can tell by her mom's expression that she doesn't really want to hear any of this.

One of the good old boys breaks off and saunters up to Dona. "Well, look what the cat drug in. Thought you was all set in your antebellum down on the beach, huh? Storm caught you good this time."

The man's attitude is combative like he knows Dona would never stop at his station if she wasn't desperate.

"It's taken us all morning to drive here from Gulfport." Measured, controlled, Dona bides her startled reaction. She needs the man's help.

"Did it now?" The man smiles. His teeth are stained brown and dark from tobacco. He eyes Dona and moves closer, boxing her between him, the Expedition, and the gas pump.

"Everything south of the railroad tracks is gone." Dona's voice sounds thin and higher than normal.

Jane-Claire steps closer and holds onto her mom's arm.

Dona continues, "I hope you and your family made out okay. Seems like the damage is pretty far inland."

"We done lost a few trees. Road signs down. That's all." The man crosses his arms and grins.

The door on the driver side of the Honda opens, but Jane-Claire keeps her eyes on the man.

"You some of the first coast dwellers to make it up here." The owner's friend ambles in and joins in the conversation. "A far piece, it is."

"We stand to make some jack on this business." The owner's grin widens, something Jane-Claire didn't think possible. Several teeth are missing in the back of his mouth.

Jane-Claire stares, face to face with people who see disaster as an opportunity to profit.

"I have cold beer . . . While it lasts. And a little ice. A few cases of granola bars I can sell." The owner gestures to several ice chests staged in a line beside the pumps.

"Sir, can we use the facilities?" Lerue joins them. He's not feeling well, but he stands as tall as he can manage. He smiles at the good ole boys. "I'm about to pop."

"Sorry, son. But you're welcome to take a piss over yonder." The men back off and the owner points to pine trees clustered alongside the station.

Lerue rubs his eyes and strays toward the trees.

"Lerue," Dona stares at her son. "I don't think so."

He looks back over his shoulder at mom and throws down one pointed stare. No more objections.

Dona redirects and turns back to the owner.

Jane-Claire winces at the size of the wad he has stuffed in his cheek.

"Can we get some gas? We'll pump it ourselves," Dona asks politely.

Jane-Claire holds her mom's arm and rests her head on her shoulder.

The owner's friend laughs and points at Jane-Claire. "I can sure tell you're the baby."

Jane-Claire straightens, mad as a hornet.

"We ain't open, lady. We just out here trying to sell what we can."

Dona is dazed. "I have cash if that helps." She touches her purse.

"Hmph, unless money can generate electricity, your cash is no good." Both men laugh.

"How much for the granola bars?" Dona pulls a twenty-dollar bill from her wallet.

"How 'bout that there?" The owner snatches the twenty-dollar bill from Dona's hand then takes his time about getting a family size box of oats and honey granola bars from a case next to the ice chests.

He shoves the box into Dona's arms.

She is speechless.

The owner doesn't care. "Supply and demand. That's the American way."

"That's price gouging. You owe us change." Jane-Claire erupts. "You're nothing but a Grima Wormtongue, ready to sell out anything for money. And don't think we won't report you to the police for this."

Jane-Claire's Grima Wormtongue reference stumps the good ole boys because they don't know what the heck she means by it. They're not *Lord of the Rings* aficionados, but her references to price gouging and police register.

They squint... hard.

Dona interrupts Jane-Claire's tear. "Thank you, gentlemen." She uses the term loosely. "Jane Claire!" She pats her daughter's fury down and pulls her in the direction of the cars.

Head down and with both hands holding his stomach, Lerue stumbles back toward the Honda.

Suddenly, a car skids into the gravel at the entrance of the gas station. All the windows in the late model tank are blown out and dings that resemble machine gun bullets riddle the side and hood. The car is loaded with passengers and skids to a stop.

An extended Hispanic family, all ages and sexes, pop from the doors and windows.

"Get the hell out of here." The good ole boy owner uses both arms to wave the family off. "This ain't no charity stop." He snarls at them.

His friend shrills a high pitch whistle and points to the road. "Keep going."

Jane-Claire seizes the box of granola bars from Dona and runs toward the car.

What looks like a hundred different arms and hands reach out to her. The case of granola bars is sucked into the mass of humanity.

The family signals their thanks and drive off.

Both good ole boys sneer at Jane-Claire.

Dona steps in. She pulls a second twenty dollar bill out of her wallet and throws it at the men.

She grabs a second case of granola bars and Jane-Claire's arm then hauls both to the Passport.

"Mom, that light thing with my eyes, that sparkling. I don't feel good." The driver's door of the Honda is not doing a great job of holding Lerue upright. He literally looks green, and his eyes are half-mast.

Dona stands with her back to the men.

Jane-Claire keeps a lookout.

"There's no place to stay here. We have to at least get to Birmingham . . . Do you think you can make it?" Dona pushes Lerue's damp curls out of his face.

His answer is irrefutable.

Lerue bends over and vomits, barely missing mom's shoes.

Dona balances the granola bars under one arm and supports Lerue's forehead with her hand.

Jane-Claire has a brilliant idea. Best all day. She looks at her mom, "Let me drive."

Dona ignores her offer. She throws the case of granola bars on the front seat of the Passport and fishes a pill from a bubble pack inside a remote pocket of her purse.

She grabs a half-drunk bottle of water and hands it with the pill to Lerue. Glass nuggets from the broken windshield stick to the back of her shirt.

Lerue moans and retches as he struggles to swallow the pill.

"Do you want to get there or what?" Jane-Claire gets in Dona's face,

Dona shakes her head and opens her mouth to say something then stops. She sighs before she starts again. "Jane-Claire, any other day. Any other time, I'd never think to let you drive."

Of course. Jane-Claire already knows this.

"No." Lerue's bleary eyes implore his mom. "But my car. Do I have to go with her?"

Dona helps him into the Passport's passenger seat. "With a learner's permit, a licensed driver has to be in the car." Survival logic has a universe all its own.

"Jeez, so I'm the sacrifice?" Jane-Claire worries that Lerue will block her plan, but he gives up pretty quick. He's feeling that bad, so he pulls his legs inside the car, and slams the door as a final protest.

"Jane-Claire, I'd never forgive myself." Dona gives her a hard look. "What if something happens?"

Jane-Claire knew she was going to say this and she's ready for it. She looks straight into her mom's eyes. "Mom, something did happen. I believe we'll look back at this as one of our finest hours." Gotcha. Her mom loves Churchill.

Jane-Claire takes the Passport keys from Dona's hand and gets in the driver's seat.

She drives the Passport by herself. There's no side seat

driving from Lerue. He took that migraine pill and is completely passed out the entire rest of the trip.

Jane-Claire stays in the middle lane once they hit the interstate, and she goes a little less than five miles over the speed limit to follow Dona.

Through the rural Mississippi landscape where everything looks like shit, this isn't a problem. Jane-Claire drives steadily and gives up looking at the gas gauge.

Either empty in Lerue's Honda doesn't really mean empty, or God grants a miracle that day because the SUV chugs on until they reach the Alabama border.

At the boundary, there are suddenly no lines for gas, no mobs at the grocery store, as if the tragedy that occurred in Mississippi and Louisiana stopped at the state line.

They reach a gas station where everyone is courteous and friendly. Someone even buys the gas for them. Another person brings drinks and offers snacks gratis. Life is totally different. People act human.

Dona and Jane-Claire use a sparkling clean restroom. They leave Lerue asleep in the car with the windows rolled down and aren't afraid that anyone will kill him.

Dona tells Jane-Claire that she's going to try to take the bypass around Birmingham to avoid the traffic downtown and to try to stay close. She checks Jane-Claire in her rearview mirror as they take off.

Jane-Claire waves and gives a thumbs up then checks Lerue. He's still breathing.

At first, she grips the steering wheel as if she'll float away if she let go. Before today, she only drove on the interstate once and that was to get on then get off at the next exit.

Going through Birmingham, Jane-Claire faces several challenges. First, she'd never been through Birmingham before. She didn't know if the exit to Huntsville would be a right exit, a left exit, or what lane to get in?

The traffic ramps up, and although she remembers her mom distinctly saying that she is going to take a road that doesn't go through downtown, she suddenly is driving between skyscrapers.

Is Mom taking the right way?

Jane-Claire decides to go with the flow and sticks to the mangled Expedition in front of her like glue. One advantage to the Expedition being wrecked was that no one wants to get close to it. Small favors.

A second challenge is that Lerue never let her drive his Honda before. Her experience was limited to the driver's education car, a sea foam green Taurus with the forest green interior. The Taurus isn't as high or big. The Passport is a definite upgrade.

Jane-Claire negotiates a lane change and a barrage of people cutting and merging to try to block her off. Then she makes up her mind that no one is getting between her and her mom. Period. Once she makes that clear, no one does, but she is in both-hands-on-the-wheel driving mode, for sure.

She turns north onto Interstate 65 and she can feel the adrenaline calm a little. Traffic thins out and there's not quite so much lane changing back and forth. She gets in a groove, a more kick-it-to-cruise-control type of driving.

The mountains and hills around Cullman still make the ride interesting and much easier to track behind her mom on the last part of the trip.

They make one stop at a McDonald's for a coke. Dona motions to Jane-Claire and she follows her blinker signals to know when to get off.

The whole drive would have been easier with cellphones, which she points out to her mom at the golden arches.

Then they drive into Huntsville. Jane-Claire finds it more than weird to be going back to a city that she hasn't been to in a long time, but still is the place where she was born.

She recognizes city landmarks and places more from stories than reality, and she tries to piece the memories together in quick succession as they drive in.

They cruise into Huntsville, straight to the hospital.

Yes, Mom wants Lerue checked out since he hit his head on the rafter.

Dad dismissed serious injury the night before but, mom is frantic and isn't convinced that his headache is just a migraine and not a sign of a concussion.

The emergency room visit takes the last of her cash and proves dad was right.

Lerue has a migraine and no concussion, but the emergency physician does invite Lerue to apply to the exclusive private school and play on their soccer team.

EIGHT

Sweet Home Alabama

Because of the stop at the hospital, they arrive at Kit and Martin Jones's house close to sunset. The house is custom-built, set on a large lot in an expensive, exclusive part of town.

The architect must have loved Frank Lloyd Wright because he designed the house to blend with the natural scenery, which is hilly with a lot of limestone boulders. A pebble driveway circles in front and goes down the back and side.

Mom's Expedition rattles to a stop in front of the main entrance, an oriental red door with brass rings circling the center. Jane-Claire parks the Passport behind her. Dona exits and stretches with fatigue.

The seven hour drive has taken them sixteen hours, but Jane-Claire focuses on success. She exits, bounds to her mom and hugs her.

"We reached Rivendell, sort of." She can't explain the tremendous sense of freedom, accomplishment, and escape. The scenery around her looks normal, and she takes comfort from that. For the moment.

"You're official over the road, O.T.R., J.C. Well done."
Exhausted, Dona's apprehension shows in the wrinkled
lines of her forehead.

Lerue emerges from the Passport's passenger side. Dark
circles ring his eyes and he did start the journey with a
black eye. He uses the Passport for support as he walks to
the house.

Kit Jones, a reed thin, 50-something, no nonsense
woman, opens the front door and immediately targets him.
"Hey kid, what you been drinkin'?"

"Migraine meds." Lerue scowls.

Kit laughs. She hugs Dona and pats her back. "Too
bad about the coast. That's what you get for moving."

Jane-Claire wants to kick the woman.

"We moved seven years ago," Dona reminds her. She
doesn't want to come here. Mason's plan is a terrible idea.

"I tried to wait for you. I'm heading out to feed the
horses. Mind making dinner? I have leftovers for beef
stroganoff." Kit walks past them.

Dona is a New Orleans cook and beef stroganoff is not
in her repertoire. She never makes something like this, but
between dad and now Kit, she is run over by the bulldozer.
She's a guest and compelled to do what's asked of her. "I
guess I could, sure."

Lerue catches mom's eye. He sticks his finger in his
mouth and pretends to wretch. Since Jane-Claire and
Dona have recent memory of him doing that, they immediately get the picture.

"Just follow my recipe. We don't like spicy foods around
here." Kit throws her blurb and trucks off to feed half a
dozen horses waiting patiently in their stalls.

Dona looks as if she's been punched.

Jane-Claire hangs close to her and holds her arm.

Martin Jones, a spindly man with a depreciating style,

exits the house and waves his arms wide in welcome. "Don't start like that Kit. They just got here."

Yes, they did. They got her message loud and clear. They aren't wanted. They're an obligation. A good heart is so rare.

Martin greets the Stevens with genuine affection. He pats Lerue's back. "Let me help you with your luggage."

Lerue pulls our three backpacks from the interior of the Honda. "It's okay. This is all we have."

Jane-Claire views the Jones's house as ying and yang, the symbol of balance between opposites. From the street, the house looks like a one-story ranch style home, albeit with Frank Lloyd Wright thrown in but in reality, the house has two stories with the front half of the bottom floor built into the sloping terrain of the hillside.

The ying and yang element screams louder on the inside where there's no balance at all.

The top floor has a museum quality about it in a 'don't touch it' sense like, "Yes, there is a couch and I guess maybe you can sit on it" kind of vibe.

Jane-Claire has the feeling that every time she sits or lies down on the bed that she needs to smooth out the wrinkles and remake it when she gets up, and she means the full treatment with the comforter up over the pillows and the pillow shams in place.

"Don't mess with it" is the operating agenda. "You can be in here but if you move something it has to go right back to where it was." That's what living here is like.

The downstairs open basement area is the yang and the place is a complete wreck. This beautiful upscale house in Huntsville is really two completely different houses, and that fact reflects the terrible struggle going on within the walls.

Jane-Claire, her mom, and Lerue trail after Martin into

the foyer, a large formal space with a mix of oriental and modern Danish style furniture. A few toys on the floor are a big hint that a baby lives here, a subfamily within Kit and Martin's family.

Dona takes note. Her eyebrows pinch together. Her mouth sets. She's not a happy camper.

Martin ushers them into a rectangular family room filled with leather sofas, a coffee table and end tables made of glass.

Windows line the far wall with a view straight out into the tops of trees. The slope the house is built on is that steep, and the foliage from the canopy of trees makes the house very dark.

"Brittany and Randy are set up in the basement, just until they can save enough for an apartment, mind you." Martin's comment is not intended for the Stevens but directed at Brittany and Randy sitting on the floor in front of the television. His words bounce off the couple.

Brittany Tate is Kit and Martin's twenty-one-year-old married daughter.

She sits in front of the television where her husband, Randy Tate, a wiry twenty something low-life, plays a violent video game.

Payton, Brittany and Randy's one-year old son tests his steps along the edge of the coffee table.

He fusses and throws anything within his reach from the table to the floor. He's hungry, sleepy, or both. The baby has a certain Lerue look.

Randy guzzles a beer. He looks straight at Jane-Claire and pats his thigh.

"Hey, wanna play?" He smiles and looks just like one of those good ole boys at the gas station.

Jane-Claire pretends that he's not talking to her.

Payton stumbles, falls, and bangs his head on the sharp

edge of the table. He cries. A lot.

"Crap." Brittany grabs Payton and spanks his bottom. "Stop it! Shut your hole!"

Payton kicks it into high gear and really bawls now.

Distressed, Martin throws his hands up at Brittany. "Payton just wants a little of your attention. Turn that damn TV off and take care of your son."

Dona moves like a flash. She gets ice from the freezer, puts it in a Ziploc, scoops Payton from the floor, and holds the boo-boo pack to his head before anyone can say another thing.

Then she turns at Martin. "We would've never thought to come here if…"

Martin cuts her off, shaking his head. "No, it's great you're here. I'm truly glad to see you. Kit has you and Jane-Claire in the guest room. I set up a blowup mattress for Lerue in the living room. It's no bother at all."

Lerue drops the backpacks to the floor and takes Payton from Dona.

Jane-Claire can tell he's thinking of Michael, and sadness overwhelms her. She picks up the few toys allowed upstairs off the floor.

Dona returns to the kitchen. "We appreciate your hospitality, Martin."

Jane-Claire bites her tongue. Hospitality. This is pure torment, and they've only been here five minutes. She wants to let loose.

Dona looks at Jane-Claire. She can't. Understood.

"I'll get dinner started." What else can mom do? She obeys the orders she's been given.

Randy makes Jane-Claire really uncomfortable. His eyes bore through her clothes.

Brittany settles next to "her man" as Jane-Claire later learns she likes to call him. Anything but. Brittany's the only person Jane-Claire can think of who can be enthralled in a video game that she's not even playing.

Jane-Claire thinks of her dad. He would've never sent them here into the maelstrom of the personal hurricane hitting the Jones family right this very second.

This family has a beautiful home with nothing on the first floor out of place, and yet they are falling apart. Everyone has troubles, problems, issues. No one is immune.

JANE-CLAIRE SOMEHOW MAKES it through the weekend to Labor Day, which she dreads because Kit promises to take them to an outdoor picnic and concert at Big Spring Park.

The city center surrounds a natural spring that spills from a sheer rock cliff formed from the porous limestone prevalent in Madison County. The lush park offers green space and small lakes joined by a canal.

A bandstand, decked out in patriotic bunting, stands at the center of an open field used as a picnic area.

Kit parades the Stevens like spoils of war through the jovial crowd lounging on the grass. Food is everywhere, and everyone is smiling.

The scene looks ridiculous and hurtful.

Jane-Claire wants to scream at these people, "Why aren't you helping? Don't you realize what just happened? Have you heard? People need your help!"

But instead, she lugs Payton and she's glad to have him to hold onto.

Lerue carries two three-foot long subway sandwiches piled high with meats and cheeses. The sandwiches look a little obscene. They can't possibly eat it all.

Martin and Brittany swing the picnic basket between

them.

Dona walks alongside Kit and tries to discuss school, another reason why Jane-Claire doesn't want Labor Day to come. School starts tomorrow whether she likes it or not. Lerue and Jane-Claire both regard high school as punching a card or looking at a clock. School is a waste of time because they have other interests. They can't wait until they finish.

Kit wants them to go to the Catholic High School since Martin's mother is a founding donor. She dragged them on a tour last Friday afternoon.

There may have been a slight chance, but when the principal boasted that he felt sure he could get Lerue and Jane-Claire uniforms to wear the first day, they knew the school was a no go and they let mom know about it.

"Over our dead bodies" was the term used. Mom agreed without further discussion which left Kit peeved all weekend. However, Lerue and Jane-Claire's insistence now put Dona in a position to have to rely on Kit's help in enrolling them in the public Huntsville High.

Lerue and Jane-Claire have been out of school a week and once disrupted, a routine is hard to reestablish.

Jane-Claire doesn't want to go back to any school because she doesn't know what's going to happen next. The whole effort seems pointless.

And Lerue just wants senior year to be over.

"Mason wants me to register the kids over at Huntsville High tomorrow." Dona chases and skips to stay next to Kit and avoid stepping on picnickers.

Kit frowns, "I'll get the deed to the house from the safety deposit box in the morning. You sure about this?"

"Thank you. I know it's a hassle, but the school says they need verification of address." The city has agreed to enroll "displaced" students into school if an apartment or house is rented in the school zone, or if a student is staying with a family within the school zone boundary.

"You need to see if your insurance will pay for an apartment." It had only been a few days, but Kit makes it plain that their stay is temporary, and she doesn't want to hear any additional news or stories from the Gulf.

"I will. I'll get on it." Dona glances back at Lerue. "College applications."

Lerue ignores her comment and acts as if he didn't hear mom. Guys can do that and get away with it. Sometimes.

Dona is fixated on Lerue's college applications as a symbol of the future which of course, is only true in relation to Lerue, who has his own ideas on the subject which he doesn't share with his mom or Jane-Claire.

"Mom." Jane-Claire warns her that Lerue doesn't want to hear anything she has to say on the subject.

Kit leads the Stevens to a crowded area just to the left of center stage. She insists on spreading the double wide plaid picnic blanket to the limit.

Families on each side press closer together and scuffle to adjust to the invasion.

Jane-Claire can't believe she picks this front and center place. Couldn't she have found something less conspicuous on the side?

She lowers Payton down on the blanket and helps divest Lerue of the sandwiches. She and Dona arrange the picnic. They all settle on the plaid blanket.

"Here goes. I got y'all these buttons. Thought they say it all." Kit pulls three small round objects from the picnic basket.

She tosses the buttons which read, "I've survived damn near everything."

Are the buttons supposed to make them feel better or

just piss them off?

Lerue and Jane-Claire stare at Dona. They're waiting for a signal to attack.

"The jury's still out on that one." Dona forces a smile and pins the button on her shirt. She nods to Lerue and Jane-Claire. Stand down.

Feeling like complete idiots, they pin the buttons to the front of their T-shirts.

Dona cuts the mega sandwiches which will help them "button it" like nothing else.

Jane-Claire manages to get Payton, who usually only eats French fries, to eat.

A country band sets up onstage.

"J.C., our Supper Club meets on the third Thursday of the month. Britt usually cleans up to earn a little extra spending money. The other girl who helps serve can't work this month. Want to help?" Kit is so jovial that Jane-Claire is immediately suspicious.

"Sure, I'll be happy to." J.C. is a title reserved for family and close friends. She's irritated because this woman is neither. If Kit hadn't called her that, she would not have been distracted into agreeing so easily. Jane-Claire has no idea what she's getting into, but it can't be good.

Brittany lounges on the blanket and keeps pushing into Lerue. She rolls over on her back and throws pieces of potato chips at him.

Lerue laughs and feeds them to Payton. He doesn't get it, but Jane-Claire knows flirting when she sees it, and so does Dona.

"Mama, I need a car seat for my car, so I won't have to load the only one we have in and out between the two cars," Brittany asks Kit, like a little girl wanting a new doll.

"It'd be easier on us all, Kit," Martin chimes in.

Jane-Claire is confused. Why doesn't he just buy Brittany a car seat? He's got a million-dollar house.

Kit is the center of attention and she's loving it. "Ask the sperm donor. Let him get it. It's his damn son." She waves to friends who had the good graces to settle on the edge of the crowd.

Jane-Claire scoops ice into her red plastic cup. Then the Master of Ceremony taps the live mic, she startles and flips toward the stage.

"Before we get started, our country has recently suffered the biggest natural disaster in our history. If any refugees are with us tonight, I'm asking you to please stand." The Master of Ceremony waves his hands out to the crowd.

Jane-Claire wants to die right then and there. She wants to sink into the earth and be done with it, never to be heard from again.

Kit yanks at Dona's arm and pushes her shoulder. "Go on, get up! Here's some!" Kit looks to the Master of Ceremonies and points to Dona.

Dona stands to shut Kit up, and Lerue and Jane-Claire can't let her do that alone. They stand with her.

People clap and smile as if they did something worthy of applause, but the only explanation that comes to Jane-Claire's mind, the only thing she can think of, is that they're clapping to show their relief. The audience is just super glad that whatever disaster it was didn't happen to them.

A group of kids standing near a brick planter wave to Lerue.

"Who are they?' Jane-Claire whispers to him.

"Kids from kindergarten. This is so weird." His face is expressionless.

Jane-Claire feels like she's floating, like none of this is real, and she's trapped in a nightmare.

Some people pass money over. Kit collects it.

A woman nearby raises her hand as if she's praying. "Bless your heart. Just bless your little heart."

Dona takes Jane-Claire's hand. She doesn't like that catch-all Southern phrase. You never know what it really means. The woman's probably saying, "F… You."

Lerue picks Payton up to head to the duck pond. Jane-Claire is sorry that Brittany doesn't have two kids.

Pity and charity set them apart. And know what?

Jane-Claire doesn't like it. Maybe Payton's shoe caught her hand, or the edge of the plastic cup. Or maybe Jane-Claire's temper took over but suddenly the cup of melting ice in her hand tips and showers over Kit. She squeals and shoots a dagger look at J.C. who shrugs then smiles.

THAT NIGHT, Jane-Claire tries to get to sleep in the guest room at the Jones's house. A nightlight on the bedside table on her mom's side casts shadows on the walls.

Some people try to help. Martin and Kit are letting them stay in their house. The situation is not convenient or easy for them.

Mom's friend in Oregon sent a laptop computer that they desperately need. Another friend in Shreveport sent a check for a thousand dollars.

Others send clothes, cards, gift certificates. They do it quietly with no fanfare.

Jane-Claire is so wound up that she wonders if she'll ever sleep again. Why make a show of helping? Why not figure out what is really needed?

Dona sits in bed beside her, cell phone to her ear.

Night is the only time that she can get a call through to the insurance adjusters.

She'll get a claim number then a message during the

day that the number has been changed so she ends up always having to call back. The whole process is a big runaround.

Dona is in a near panic and talks in the hushed whisper that makes Jane-Claire cringe. Her dad has only called once. He yelled at mom the whole time.

"But I can't meet with you at the house. I evacuated. I'm several hundred miles north. There's no place to stay there. My husband is still in Gulfport. He may be able to meet with you if we can set up a time. Yes, I'll hold." Dona sighs and leans back against the headboard.

Jane-Claire stirs in the bed. Mom pats her back. "Sorry J.C., this is the only time I can get through. I'm so sorry."

Jane-Claire cuddles next to her mom and looks around Kit's guest room.

Everything is in its place. Nothing is broken.

She can't help but think of all they left behind. Everything in their house that was carefully placed. Everything in her room that meant so much to her. All of it is gone. She hasn't cried.

Not before tonight. Tears turn on.

Her mom puts her arm around her.

Jane-Claire wipes her eyes. "I write to Natalie. I send two copies. One to her house and one to the hospital. I don't know if she gets them. I don't even know where she is."

"Sweetheart, we haven't had any mail delivery since the storm. The post office was damaged. Dad's tried to go stand in line but . . . He couldn't wait that long."

Dona tilts her head back and ponders implications. "Late payments, that's all I need. Our credit score's going to be trashed. I'm trying to remember everything and take care of it."

"I gave my journal to Nat."

Mom covers the phone receiver and looks at her daughter. "Did she lose it? I didn't say anything before, but you should have given the violin back. Why did y'all even do something stupid like that?"

And then, she's back on the phone again.

"Yes, I have the policy number right here. Is it possible to see an agent in a different town? What? An inventory? My daughter filmed the contents. Would that work?"

"It's all gone. Everything's gone." Tears pour. Jane-Claire can't stop them. She can't help it. This is the first time she really says that, and she breaks down and cries into her mom's shoulder.

"Excuse me?" Dona sits straighter. She juggles comforting Jane-Claire and dealing with the insurance adjuster at the same time. "You'll just have to take my word for it? Have an adjuster go by the house. Compare the layout with the video. Do you really have time for that? No, I don't have sales receipts for every piece of furniture I bought in the last 20 years." Dona breathes deep to control her mounting anger.

Jane-Claire drifts into the hinterland of grief and walks through the dense fog of what used to be her bedroom.

"My Legolas cutout. My Inuyasha poster. My white iron bed. The brass knobs. We looked so hard for those. We bought them in New Orleans, remember? My swimming medals." She catalogues her room down to the smallest detail.

"That's a lot of 'my', J.C." Dona breaks off with the insurance adjuster to point that out.

Then just as quickly back to the phone. "Sorry, I was talking to my daughter. No, I'm fine. May I please speak to your supervisor? Do you have a supervisor there I could talk to?"

"My American Girl doll. My bike. The ping pong

table. Our volleyball net." Jane-Claire continues.

The call drops. Mom glares at the phone.

"No! It took me two hours to get through to them!" She throws the phone into the covers and hugs her daughter. "Go ahead. Name it all. Every little thing." Dona scrunches down in the bed and settles next to her.

"My clothes. My first pointe shoes. My ballet costumes." Jane-Claire cries so hard that she can hardly talk.

"The corner cabinets in the living room. My Paw-Paw built them, and they broke into splinters." Dona adds to the litany.

"My autograph dog. My yearbooks." Jane-Claire blows her nose on a Kleenex her mom hands her.

"Mine too. Grandmother's mahogany hope chest. She brought it with her all the way on a ship from France. All my wedding silver was inside. Oh, gees, my wedding pictures. They're all gone." That's as far as Dona goes. She doesn't name anything after that.

"My journal. What happened to my journal?" Jane-Claire dissolves into her tears.

"At least you have your video camera. That's your real prize." Dona holds her close.

Jane-Claire hasn't been able to bring herself to touch her video camera. Everything lately is too real and too terrible. She put the camera in its case next to Natalie's violin in Kit's guest room closet and shut the door. Her video camera is one of her few belongings that was not destroyed in the storm, and she almost hates that she still has it.

Encircled in her mother's arms in the dimly lit but perfectly neat guest room, she convicts herself of cheating in the bargain with Natalie. Her journal is precious to her, but her video camera is her treasure.

NINE

Displaced

Huntsville is in north Alabama, near the Tennessee state line and the weather is four seasons, at least compared to Gulfport. The sky is clear and so bright that it doesn't even look real; and the air is crisp, even chilly.

Dona and Jane-Claire stand in a humongous line that winds through the inside and out into the parking lot of the Huntsville Baptist Church Hospitality Center. They've been in line for two hours and just cleared the door.

In Gulfport, Mason plans to go straight from night shift to stand in a FEMA line. The Federal Emergency Management Authority provides trailers and the Red Cross gives aid to refugees, which is what the Stevens family is now officially known as.

Dona is not sure that this is the best thing to do, but Mason insists if he is going to stand in line then she should try to get any aid offered as well. Tit for Tat. Lerue watches Payton and Jane-Claire couldn't let her mom come here alone.

Refugees and volunteers fill the noisy meeting hall, and

it's easy to tell them apart. A certain hysterical fear flickers in the eyes of refugees that has nothing to do with race, dress, or cleanliness. Some people look like they haven't showered or changed since the storm.

Dona and Jane-Claire are clean enough, but their eyes reflect shock and anxiety. They just don't look right. Jane-Claire, Dona, and most of the people in line have tunnel vision. They don't even notice the beautiful day.

A woman in back of them lets her three children run wild.

"This is going to take forever." Dona fidgets, breathes faster than necessary, and she's sweating as if she just ran a marathon. Not normal.

Hypervigilance is a classic post-traumatic stress symptom.

Jane-Claire read about it on Kit's computer, and the strain is visible in the face of every refugee this morning.

A long circular piece of elastic string beckons from the floor near an outside window and Jane-Claire runs to retrieve it. She learned string games a long time ago.

She starts with cat's cradle. Dona's restless movement ceases. Jane-Claire makes Jacob's ladder next, then witch's broom and spider web after a few failed attempts. She finally gets it right. Her hands remember what her brain cannot.

Soon, the feral children of the woman in back of them and several more sit on the floor in front of Jane-Claire. They are fascinated, like she's always been by the intricate patterns of the woven string. Parents in line watch.

Jane-Claire creates an oasis of peace where smiles prevail while they all wait. Her audience breaks into spontaneous applause after she makes each string figure.

· · ·

MEANWHILE, Mason stands stuck in a ponderous line at the National Guard Armory in Mississippi. Working a string of nights, he narrows his eyes in the morning glare like a nocturnal animal out of its element. His scrubs hang from him. Weight melts in the face of extreme stress.

Anxiety and fear rev the body's metabolism so high that calories burn as easily as igniting a match.

"Hey, you remember me?" A woman in back of Mason bounces a baby on her hip.

Mason looks over his shoulder. He's oblivious and has no idea that the woman's talking to him.

He's worked nonstop since the storm. Twelve to sixteen hours on duty and the rest of the day throwing in some food and trying to sleep. Exhaustion etches deep lines in his face.

Mason can hardly stay awake much less be civil and focus.

"You the doc caught my baby?" The woman smiles.

Mason nods. "They grow up fast, huh?"

"Yes, sir. Your house wiped?" The woman bonds with Mason since he delivered her child.

Mason sweeps his hand through the air. "Yeah. Sure was."

"Mine too. I need me a trailer." She harps the common theme.

Mason nods back at the long line. "Don't we all?"

When he finally gets into the old warehouse that's been converted into an official FEMA processing center, the air is deadly hot and two massive fans roar in the background.

Mason collapses into a seat before an application officer, and hands the man his application that he filled out between patients the night before.

"Sorry, sir. You're not essential personnel." The man looks to the next person in line as he says this to Mason.

"What?" Mason blinks to pry his eyes open as he endeavors to process what he's just been told. "I'm not essential personnel?"

"You're not on the list." The application officer clears his throat and looks away, unable to make eye contact.

"Then who the hell is on the list?" Mason shouts then backs off.

"City officials. Their families. You have the right to appeal the decision. I have the forms."

"Forms. You can take your forms and shove them up your ass." Mason flat loses it. He jumps to his feet. "I'm one of only ten ER docs between Mobile and New Orleans. I have no place to stay. I need a trailer yesterday. I sent my family away. I stayed for my patients."

The applications officer signals for security then chuckles. "You're here because you have a job."

Mason bangs both of his hands on top of the desk. "I can get a damn job anywhere. Why do you think so many docs have left?"

He waves his arms and huffs. "Sir, I treat every person who enters the ER. I don't perform wallet biopsies to see if they have connections or money, which is precisely what you're doing here."

Two security officers grasp Mason's arms.

He shakes them off and holds his hands up. "Okay, okay. I'll leave."

"Stay cool doc." The woman with the baby who was in line with Mason sits at the next desk. "Treat him better. Lord God sees it all."

"I sure as hell hope so." Mason backs from the desk.

The family finds out about Mason's run in with security much later, but the incident throws a real monkey wrench into getting a trailer and moving back to the coast. They can't blame him. They would've been pretty hot too.

. . .

AT THE FIRST BAPTIST HOSPITALITY CENTER, Jane-Claire teaches a few of the basic string games to one of the older kids who has a talent for it, with the understanding that he passes the game along to someone else in line when his family finally gets close to the long tables used as desks at the front of the line.

Dona and Jane-Claire sit in front of a volunteer lady named Mrs. Pushin.

The woman wears heavy makeup, stylish clothes, and the Burberry scarf looped around her neck is probably the real deal. She could have at least worn jeans when everyone else looks like homeless people. Wait. They are homeless people.

Mrs. Pushin takes a lot of time to explain that she's sitting in for a Red Cross worker as part of her service obligation to Junior League.

Dona and Jane-Claire don't understand why this makes a difference to anyone except Mrs. Pushin.

Jane-Claire observes the children waiting in the line. Her string game apprentice gives her a nod and she basks in his smile. She hopes he remembers that he is more than the personal destruction he's witnessed in the past week.

She turns and looks through the window directly in back of Mrs. Pushin at her table desk to the most beautiful blue sky she has ever seen. Eureka.

Dona concentrates on what Mrs. Pushin says which is pure word salad.

"Why, I remember you and your husband. You were a member of medical auxiliary." Mrs. Pushin's hand flashes a disparaging gesture. "That organization's gone down the tubes. Too many new wives if you get my drift."

"I worked at Huntsville Ballet a number of years. I

taught your two girls. They were in my AB level and pointe class." Dona never associated socially with this woman and she never forgets her students.

"The Red Cross gift won't buy much." Mrs. Pushin hands Dona a check for twelve hundred dollars.

"The money will help with something."

"Your husband does still have his job. I know…. Why don't I take up a collection at the auxiliary? I'd be happy to organize one for you." The woman acts like this is a sudden brainstorm.

"No, please." Dona's eyes pop, her voice too loud. "That's okay, really."

"Are you planning to go back to the coast? Do you want to rebuild?" The woman's questions aren't bad in and of themselves. They just reflect a total lack of under-standing of the chaos the last week brought to their lives.

"We haven't decided. Everything's such a stir." Dona's voice is flat, and she has to search for words. What an understatement plus. When have any of them had time to think about future plans? That's part of the problem.

Mrs. Pushin points at Jane-Claire and pulls a bright pink bag from under the table. "I do have a little care package for your girl. Socks, undies, and fresh makeup."

"Thanks." Jane-Claire takes the goody bag. She is that pragmatic.

Dona stands to leave, then stops, "Wait, there's one thing. Do you have a car seat?"

Mrs. Pushin blushes. "Why, Dona, you surprise me. You and the good doctor started over?" She breaks into a mischievous smile and winks at Dona.

"Yeah. I need a car seat." Dona doesn't exactly answer her question and would count this as a sin of omission for Jane-Claire, but she goes with it just the same.

"Come with me." Mrs. Pushin gets up and leads them to the donation collection area.

They file past mounds of stinking used clothing, shoes, and random beat up furniture. People donate their dregs. The stuff looks little better than the wet detritus inside the house in Gulfport.

Mrs. Pushin stops in front of a pile of beat up boxes. She struggles to pull a car seat from under a broken playpen. The car seat is filthy and looks as if a kid lived in it.

"Thank you for your time," Dona seizes Jane-Claire hand and proceeds in full retreat.

"Wait." Mrs. Pushin follows them. "I could look for another."

Dona hauls Jane-Claire through the crowd and doesn't look back. People don't always get what they deserve, good or bad.

DONA DEFINITELY IS a glutton for punishment that day. Kit gets the necessary paperwork for her to enroll Lerue and Jane-Claire at the public high school.

Without stopping for lunch, Dona takes them straight over to the school. Lerue sits next to Dona in the hallway outside of the counselor's office. Jane-Claire paces the hall and inspects a case brimming with first place trophies, then checks out award plaques lining the walls.

Lerue looks comatose. Dona should have fed him. He is a senior this year. He practiced on Gulfport's swim team all summer, planned to play on the soccer team, and was on track to be valedictorian. He is derailed, like Jane-Claire and Dona, but with more angst.

Jane-Claire worries that changing schools may be Lerue's Waterloo.

"Why can't we just wait till Gulfport starts back? We should go home. I want to be there. Dad needs my help. I'm missing everything." He's angry and he doesn't want to go here.

Okay, that's a given, but somehow Lerue's rant reminds Jane-Claire of movies where young men yearn to go off to war, pick any of them, because they don't want to miss the experience. They're always afraid the fighting will be over before they can get there. Jane-Claire hates to point out that most wars last way longer than anyone wants them too, and most of the young men die.

"Gulfport schools might not reopen for quite a while." Dona makes her thesis statement.

Jane-Claire says a silent prayer that the Gulfport schools stay closed until Natalie's broken arm mends. She pleads for school in Gulfport to take a long recess.

"Even then, when it does open, how much work will be accomplished? You can't afford to do nothing for a year," Dona muses.

Jane-Claire knew a kid who essentially finished all his credits by senior year, so he took choir. That was his one and only course the whole year. He had a hard time stepping up his game again for his first year in college.

Lerue grunts. Mom has a point.

The problem is that mom and Lerue are exactly the same, which is good in a way because they're determined, aggressive, and go after what they want, but bad in a way because when they lock horns, the encounter is a slugfest because they're so equal. They push and fight to a dead heat draw.

"Who cares? I just want to go home. I don't want to go here. I want to be part of the recovery. I should be with Dad." Lerue can look mean when he wants to. He does, right now.

"This is temporary," Dona says this like it explains all. She's trying to move forward. Jane-Claire and Lerue understand that, but the family is in mourning. Grief demands time.

"What does that even mean? How can I live a temporary life?" Lerue hits the real point, the problem they face. There is no temporary in life. There is here and now.

"I don't know." Dona folds her hands on her lap and waits.

Jane-Claire sighs, relieved that her mom concedes. Escalation in the counselor's hallway is a bad beginning.

"But isn't everything temporary?" She flops into a seat next to her mom. She can't believe she just said this, but it's a valid question. "Or, is everything permanent because once you live the present, you can't change it?"

Dona and Lerue stare at Jane-Claire like they'd like to kill her, but they can't because the door to the counselor's office opens.

An exasperated mother and her burly son exit the counselor's office.

"You quit now, and you'll never go back." The mom warns her son in a hissing whisper. She tugs him down the hallway to the exit.

Jane-Claire watches them walk down the hall and wonders why they were privy to that conversation?

The senior counselor, a rotund grandmotherly woman, stands in her office door.

"Mrs. Stevens, I understand you're from New Orleans. Please come in." She ushers them into a cramped office with a window overlooking the front lawn of the school and gestures to a seat.

This is so surreal.

Dona and Jane-Claire crowd into the only two chairs

right in front of her desk. Lerue remains close to the office door. He looks like he's ready to jump ship.

"I am from New Orleans, but our home was in Gulfport," Dona explains as introduction.

"Gulfport took the direct hit. The eye of the storm came right over us. New Orleans just got flooded." Way to go, Lerue. Be combative right off the bat.

But Lerue is right. Gulfport took the full brunt of the storm and New Orleans got the news coverage.

Jane-Claire looks at her mom. For the first time, she considers what a double whammy this must be for her. She lost her home in Gulfport and her past in New Orleans, every school she ever went to, every house she ever lived in.

"We've already taken in more than thirty displaced students. Most are from New Orleans." Grandmother Counselor puts on a pair of readers and scans a list of student names, as if that has something to do with them.

Displaced sounds disconnected. Why doesn't the woman just go ahead and say refugees?

The high school counselor eyes Lerue. "Mr. Stevens, you are my only displaced senior. Our swim program can use you. I checked eligibility."

Lerue brightens in spite of himself. "I play soccer too."

"Well, soccer season hasn't started yet, but I also understand that you might qualify for National Merit." Grandmother Counselor has clearly discussed Lerue.

"We'll see." Lerue isn't too happy about this. He didn't mean to get such a high score in PSAT. He doesn't like the attention, but a full ride scholarship would be hard to pass up.

Grandmother Counselor turns to Jane-Claire. "And you've been difficult, young lady. I've made several exceptions for you in an effort to match your schedule. I don't want it to be unduly stressful, so I've added art and interior design. Mrs. Quintero and Mrs. Malbus asked for you. They both know your mother."

"Art?" Jane-Claire can't help it. She makes a face like she just smelled something bad. She has recent experience.

Dona's smile is genuine.

Jane-Claire is glad to see it. "Mrs. Quintero and I worked together at the ballet school. She teaches jazz. She's super talented. Her grandfather's artwork is famous. He was one of the first African American artists to be nationally recognized."

That's great and everything but Jane-Claire has to live with this woman's expert schedule matching, and this is how it really turns out.

First of all, school had been in session in Gulfport for less than two weeks, so Jane-Claire wasn't all that invested in her Gulfport schedule to begin with.

Anatomy in Gulfport is a sophomore class but a senior class at Huntsville High. The Counselor lets Jane-Claire go ahead and take the class so, her first period class is with people that will not only never be in any of her other classes but also, they never speak to her.

In ballet, there is a term for a student who is always in class but never called on or talked to. That student is a ghost and that's what Jane-Claire becomes in her anatomy class.

Then in fifth period which lines up with sophomore lunch, the Counselor schedules her to be an office aide which is also usually reserved for juniors and seniors.

That decision prevents her from going to lunch with anyone in her grade.

From the beginning, Jane-Claire's schedule segregates her from her peers. She is a ghost for most of her day.

She is an office aide with a girl who also is in her

anatomy class. The other office aide ends up being a teenage mom halfway through the year. How that helps her see some normalcy becomes something of a joke.

Then there is History class.

In Gulfport, Jane-Claire had just started World History because she took U.S. History the year before the storm. Grandmother Counselor says that World History is a freshman level class in Huntsville, and she doesn't want to put her in that, so she places her in U.S. History again. Jane-Claire takes U.S. History two times in high school and never World History in her entire high school academic career. She still has the World History text book from Gulfport which Dona made them take to do homework for classes that they would never be in again. Makes perfect sense.

And English . . . She reads *Lord of the Flies* again, but she already studied the book freshman year, so she reads it twice as required reading in high school. Jane-Claire has a very worn book of *Lord of the Flies* with lots of notes because she used it over and over in her beach film making and recreation. She calls it "The director's note version of *Lord of the Flies*."

Jane-Claire likes her anatomy teacher, until she invites a representative from University of Alabama in Huntsville to class to show the traveling "Bodies" exhibit, a cadaver thing.

The exhibit is new and had just opened in Chicago and New York at the time. People donate their bodies to science, and technicians peel back the layers. The muscles are plasticized and can stand up. Almost.

The anatomy teacher intends to inspire her students to become doctors, but the exhibit is a great example of "too much, too soon."

The anatomy classroom is a decent size conference

room with a presentation movie theater type set up, raked stadium seating and everything.

The UAH representative takes out hearts, normal lungs, and lungs that had been smoking lungs. Those are all covered in black tar stuff then she put the body parts on lunch trays that are the same color and style as actual lunch trays in the cafeteria. She passes around body parts on lunch trays in the classroom.

The whole experience is really, really bizarre.

When Jane-Claire goes to lunch, her food is served on the same type lunch tray. It reminds her of the hand she saw in the Gatorade barrel and the dead bodies on the stretchers in the echocardiography room.

Any thoughts about following in her dad's footsteps are laid to rest in anatomy class.

Grandmother Counselor is so convinced she is smart with that scheduling.

She stands at her desk and looks down at Lerue and Jane-Claire. "I'm so sorry. My son and I survived Hurricane Andrew years ago. We had to live in a trailer for quite a while till the house was rebuilt. Recovery always seems out of reach. Tragedy pushes us to the basics. Food, clothing, shelter."

Is she saying her disaster is worse? Is she comparing ruin and misfortune?

"Life is more complicated than that." Dona won't play and gives the courteous response.

"Things can always be worse." Grandmother Counselor clucks as she makes her pronouncement. "You have resources. Your husband's a physician. At least no one in your family died."

Jane-Claire looks at her mom. Lerue looks at Jane-Claire. The cliché they hear over and over. Things can always be worse.

Jane-Claire hates the phrase along with assumptions.

Their dad is a doc which to most people means he makes a lot of money, but to Jane-Claire, it only means that she listens to horribly, tragic stories at dinner and that he's not home on weekends, nights, or holidays because patients, not family, come first.

And although it is true that no one died, Jane-Claire ruminates that if they were dead, they'd never have to hear that "things could always be worse" which doesn't make what live people are going through any easier. Ugh . . . Enough.

DONA HAS two more items on her to do list that day. Jane-Claire and Lerue think she believes that if she runs fast enough, then the destruction and fear caused by what just happened to the family won't catch up with her.

Flight is winning over fight at this point.

Lerue and Jane-Claire are beat, but Dona makes a quick stop at the Wal-Mart then heads to the Huntsville Ballet.

Lerue is fine with this because he can hang in the car which is a standalone eyesore. Every place they go, people stare and point. Whatever.

Jane-Claire is too tired to take ballet class and too wired not to, but the minute they enter the studio, she's hooked.

The artistic director presents her with new leotards, tights, ballet shoes. Everything she needs has been donated by the owner of the local dance store. He invites her to dance Snow in Nutcracker and disparages that company auditions for the year have already taken place.

In another place and a different set up, maybe Jane-Claire might be disappointed, but she is relieved.

Company classes are every day and require a mindset that she doesn't have right now. She loves ballet, but she doesn't want to make it her career, and the artistic director somehow has most of the advanced class convinced that they will become dancers.

Jane-Claire dances because she enjoys it. Ballet has an intrinsic value to enjoy the present. She's as good as any of the girls in company, and she revels in the visceral pleasure of movement and the quality of the music.

None of those girls with the mind set of ballet becoming their life end up doing that. None of them. They either go to 'Bama or become Miss Auburn, or run a church group wherever, but no one enjoys class that night as much as Jane-Claire.

Mom treats them to a steak dinner, and there is something decadent and wonderful about the experience. They arrive back at Kit and Martin's late in the evening.

"Kitchen's closed." Irritated, Kit sits at the dining room table pulling her boots off.

Martin waves from the computer desk. Brittany and Randy watch television. Payton is passed out on the floor of the family room.

Lerue carries a cumbersome box ahead of Dona and Jane-Claire. Dona sneaks up behind him and snatches the Walmart receipt taped to the box's side. All is well.

"What is it?" Brittany gets up from the recliner and walks to the box.

"Open it and see." Lerue places the box on the floor.

"They were giving them out over at First Baptist and I thought of you." Dona hugs Brittany who rips the box open.

"Wow, look mom." Brittany pulls a new car seat from inside.

Randy and Kit glare at Dona. Martin beams.

Jane-Claire, Lerue, and Dona are happy. A good day, and the abnormal alert in each of them is tired enough to relax for a moment. They sleep well. Who can ask for more?

TEN

Wind or Water

———————————————

The next day, Lerue and Jane-Claire start school for the second time that year. As part of Jane-Claire's amazing schedule, she enters the Introduction to Art class with so much apprehension that she might faint. She's so awful at drawing, that she is sure that her lack of skill might poison her grade point average.

A petite African American lady with rich features and beautiful eyes greets her at the entrance to the classroom. The teacher reminds her so much of Natalie that she is struck by a palpable homesickness. She fights to contain her tears.

Mrs. Quintero escorts her into a studio classroom full of students, all staring.

Jane-Claire is convinced that the only reason she doesn't keel over is because the teacher holds her hand so tightly.

"Class, I'm proud to introduce a young girl who has courage and grit." Jane-Claire's eyes widen. She stands beside Mrs. Quintero in a stupor shock. "She's a citizen of our city, Madison County, the state of Alabama, United States of America, of our planet Earth in the Milky Way galaxy, and the universe. I see greatness and I'm so happy she's in our class because. . .." Mrs. Quintero pauses then the entire class joins with her to yell, "We're the best!"

Jane-Claire wants to run for cover.

Then applause erupts and suddenly, she repels her horrified shock like an old molting crab shell.

Mrs. Quintero guides Jane-Claire to an empty space at one of the long art tables. New art supplies and a patterned canvas storage bag wait for her.

"The class and I pitched in for your supplies. Enjoy the fresh start." The lady smiles at her.

Jane-Claire scans the class then announces her confession to Mrs. Quintero, "My artwork totally sucks."

Unfazed by her pronouncement, Mrs. Quintero declares, "I don't believe that for a minute. You're your mother's daughter. Your work will be wonderful because it's from you."

Jane-Claire looks at Mrs. Quintero as if she's crazy, because she is. But somehow, she believes her.

Sometimes kindness is all it takes. She ends up doing a lot of dance and space art projects. One of her drawings is a guy partnering a girl in ballet, and it turns out pretty legit. She puts together a black and white collage that evolves into an outline of a dancer performing a back attitude. Jane-Claire is proud of her work.

All accomplished because Mrs. Quintero believes in her. The teacher's extremely sweet, but she's also really good at keeping in line the dumb stunts of kids Jane-Claire doesn't like.

A lot of the kids at Huntsville High are very rich. One of the girls wrecks her car and the next day, she drives to school with a nicer, newer model. Then she crashes that one so bad that she and her sister wear a donut around their necks for weeks.

And then there are the guys who get brand new spruced up trucks on their birthday. They come into class and have the nerve to do dip.

One day, Mrs. Quintero calls one of them out. She's all nice and happy one minute, then in the next, she makes the guy eat the dip.

Jane-Claire has never seen a guy cry like this kid did when he's trying to swallow that awful stuff.

Mrs. Quintero never says another word about it, but no one dares do dip in her class again. She's so nice but she manages her class well.

Jane-Claire likes that because in every other class, the kids run the teacher.

But being a refugee, in the storm, displaced, whatever you want to call it, forces Jane-Claire to grow up quickly. She doesn't relate to the high school kids very well. They worry about what car they're going to get, or what dance is coming up.

Jane-Claire never folds into that mindset. She decides early on that if she's going to do something, she's going for the best possible outcome. Disaster is uncontrollable. Bad presents in its own time and place. She'll at least try to keep pace.

Meanwhile, Lerue's experience in his first class of the day is totally different. Math is his subject of choice. He's always been ahead of the curve and took calculus last year as a junior. Grandmother Counselor has no idea where to place him because university courses are his current level, and it is too late to register there for fall semester. Nothing is left for him to take in high school so primarily because swim team practice is the last period of the day, she places him in Math Seminar with Alta Morrison.

After his first class, the portly young instructor of Math Seminar, calls Lerue to the front of the classroom then waits until all the other students leave.

When they are alone, she begins the assault. "You think your refugee status puts you above our regular students?"

"No, ma'am." Lerue has no clue where this is going. He's never yet heard refugee and status put together in the same sentence.

"All assignments from the beginning of school will be completed if you are to remain in my class." Ms. Morrison tilts her head back to talk to Lerue.

Lerue is confused. Why would she have him do this? "I don't even know how long my family will be here. Besides, I took calculus last year. This class is nothing but a repeat for me. It's a placeholder." Lerue's jaw tenses. He's not big on confrontation but he will stand up for himself when provoked.

Ms. Morrison reacts negatively to his comment. She puffs to full plumage before Lerue. "You should be thankful our school took you in. Those people on the coast with their casinos and gambling, they brought God's judgment down on themselves. What do they expect condoning such sin and vice?"

"You're saying we deserved it?" Lerue is incredulous. He flashes a smile at Mrs. Morrison. "My parents never gamble. The only reason we ever hit the casinos is the buffet. The Beau has Dungeness crab every night."

"The work will be done." Ms. Morrison is one of the few people on the planet who is not swayed by an infectious smile.

Lerue contemplates the quality of her Christianity in

the face of her bigoted comment but he keeps his focus. "I don't need this class to graduate. I'm planning on taking BC calculus at the University in the spring... If I'm still here. Since you make me feel so welcome, I hope I'm not."

Lerue decides that he better not say anything else. He turns and walks out while Ms. Morrison is still talking like a clucking hen. He goes straight to Grandmother Counselor to withdraw from the class, and he hopes that is the end of the matter.

DONA ISN'T HAVING much luck either. Today is one giant frustration bomb, which is a fair description of early attempts to recover after a natural disaster.

She sits before a Good Neighbor insurance agent at his cluttered desk in a dated office that was once part of a fifties style rancher.

"Rent for an apartment is available under a homeowner's policy in Alabama. We're sure we can help. We're just waiting for authorization."

Dona doesn't see a "we" sitting there, only a single agent, a middle-aged mush mouth of a man who always wears brown. He uses his shoulder to hold a receiver of an old rotary phone to his ear.

Dona tries to distract her racing thoughts by speculating whether her children have ever seen a rotary phone in action.

When his secretary, an older woman in a worn suit, comes into the office to bring papers to the agent, she plucks a size sticker from Dona's blouse.

Embarrassed, Dona flusters. She had to buy the sage green jacket and black pants from Walmart the day before. She literally had nothing to wear.

"I don't believe anyone saw it." The woman pats Dona's shoulder. "Bless your heart."

The springs in the leather chair Dona sits in are broken, and the longer she sits, the more she sinks. So, she is put in the uncomfortable position of looking up like a small child at the secretary.

"Thanks. I thought we'd only be gone a couple of days. I didn't pack much. It's hard to shop for new clothes. Jane-Claire won't." Dona looks away. She's talking too damn much because she's nervous.

The insurance agent glances up from the phone. "My Grammy on my pappy's side . . . Her house burned to the ground one Sunday when she was at meeting. Terrible. I was only a child and I remember so well. The family Bible. All the photographs." The insurance agent nods as he tells the story.

Dona listens then tries to get him back on target. "I'd like to get an apartment as soon as possible. I feel like I'm imposing on my friends."

"Oh, honey, don't think twice about that," The man waves a dismissive hand in the air. "Your friends'll be able to take you off of their income tax this year. The president announced it yesterday. I'd put you up in my house if I had room."

He stops and redirects to the voice on the phone, "Yes, sir. Oh, I see. That's too bad. Glad I called to check. Thank you, sir." The insurance flips the receiver back onto the phone cradle. He leans to the desk and brings his hands together.

Dona reads the man's body language. It looks bad.

"I'm afraid your rent request is declined. Policies on Mississippi Gulf coast are exempt from that provision. It's not part of your homeowner's policy. Of course, that's why you purchased separate flood and wind."

"Thank you. I appreciate your time," Water or wind? The debate about the original cause of damage rages and policies pay only after adjusters duke it out. No money for rent. She's playing a rigged game.

ELEVEN

Making Sense of Aftermath

Jane-Claire is an office aide in third period with a senior who wears layers of make-up and never says a word to her. Until today.

"Those little Guido guys who wear the Catholic school uniforms all the time. They hang with your brother. They were his teammates at Jesuit?"

She pops gum as they walk down the hall to deliver newsletters to the teacher's lounge. "I didn't know you were from New Orleans."

"What garbage." Jane-Claire slows down but refuses to look at the girl.

Several kids from New Orleans are spectacularly obnoxious. The two brothers in question are fanatically proud that they attend Jesuit High School and insist on wearing their Catholic school uniforms every day as if they are still there.

Huntsville High is a public school, so this makes quite the statement.

"You went to Dominican? I hear that's the Ritz. Ann Rice went to Dominican." This girl has never acknowledged Jane-Claire's existence to this point. "Why doesn't Lerue wear his uniform? Was it destroyed in the hurricane?"

"He doesn't have a uniform. He never went to school with them." Jane-Claire doesn't even know where to begin. Lerue is big friends with the Guidos. They make him laugh and they're teammates now because they're all on swim team together. Beyond that. . ..

"Seriously?" The girl nudges Jane-Claire as if they're BFFs. "Tell me the truth."

No one ever gets the story right. People assume. One group thinks that they moved to Huntsville because of their dad's work and that's that. Others don't care enough to ask why, how, or where from. Some act like they want to know, but they assume they're from New Orleans, ask a couple of clueless questions since they're not from the city, then move on. A couple of people want a little bit more information. They'll ask about the storm and start to listen, but they don't want the whole story, just a juicy tidbit. The worst thing is that when Jane-Claire tries to tell the truth to whoever is streaming this made up stuff, no one believes her, and the urban legend stands.

"Yeah, Dominican is Jesuit's sister school. It takes a lot to even get in." Jane-Claire found that much out. She starts walking again. The stack of newsletters is heavy. "Lerue's just broken hearted because his uniforms were destroyed in the hurricane. He doesn't have a girlfriend, if that's what you're asking." Jane-Claire's smile is tight, closed but the upperclassman cohort smiles broadly. That's just what she wanted to know.

THE STEVENS HAVE BEEN in Huntsville almost three weeks now. Jane-Claire writes Natalie every day. She asks her dad to check up on her, but he never has any news. Time moves on. Another hurricane devastates Houston and the west coast of Louisiana.

Dona is a scarecrow. Her clothes hang from her. She spends half the night talking to insurance adjusters, and half the day driving around and trying to stay out of Kit's way. Jane-Claire can't remember the last time she saw her asleep, and they do share the same bed.

Jane-Claire tosses all this around in her mind while she sits in the library. The room is large, bright and cheerful, except that she's sitting here with Lerue waiting for the refugee support group to start. The support group may mean well, but it's kind of sick.

Most of the kids are African American from the inner city and ninth ward of New Orleans. Jane-Claire and Lerue gather that's not the best place to be from real quick. The Jesuit brothers huddle around Lerue for protection since he's bigger than they are. Jane-Claire figures they must know more about these kids than they do.

At first, Grandmother Counselor tries to run the group, but she keeps acting like she's a psychologist and not a school counselor. A bona fide counselor from the hospital takes over pretty quick. The woman looks like she's in a sorority and runs the group like an illness support group, as if they all have cancer, or like they caught a terrible disease called "refugee."

Early on, it becomes obvious that she's going to use anything they say to write a paper for a journal or a report to justify that she did something, or to make the hospital look good. She listens no better than anyone else. She just wants snippets of the scoop. A good sampling.

The Crisis Counselor is a young woman in her mid-twenties, a human relations intern at the hospital. She stands behind a podium at the front of the room. "Suicidal thoughts are normal in your situation. Heightened awareness, social withdrawal, anxiety, insomnia are just a few of the symptoms. Is anyone having such thoughts? No fear. No judgement in this group. Speak up."

Dead Silence. The students sit while the crisis counselor waits for them to fall apart. She seems disappointed that they all just look bored. The counselor decides to take a chance and asks a question in desperation.

"What is the hardest thing, the absolute most difficult problem you've encountered since relocating?" That's what they call it because it makes evacuating sound voluntary. LOL!

One of the New Orleans kids, an African American boy six times Jane-Claire's size blurts out, "English." His name is D'wayne Duplancais.

Jane-Claire perks. That's something she can work with, so she enlists Lerue and the Jesuit brothers and turns the support group into a tutoring group. It's nice to get out of other classes for a minute, to talk with people who sort of understand what they're going through because they are too. They actually help some of the students who aren't doing so hot.

Jane-Claire tutors English and she volunteers Lerue for math. The Jesuit boys take whatever is left, and the refugee group becomes pretty fun after that.

JANE-CLAIRE SITS with D'wayne a week later. "Was your test score better?"

D'wayne shrugs. He's not a man of many words.

"Is that a yes?" She presses. D'wayne holds up two fingers and nods.

"Two points better?" She finds prompts the best way to communicate with D'wayne.

"Two grades." The gentle giant smiles, lovely to see. They exchange a high five.

"That's awesome! A great start." Jane-Claire takes an envelope from her purse and passes it to D'wayne under the table. "Don't make a big deal out of this but I asked mom. Check engine lights are there for a purpose. Get your mom to fix the car." D'wayne and his mom stay with a hostile uncle. His mom is recovering from a stroke she suffered the week after the storm and their car is on the skids.

"Thanks." D'wayne fist bumps Jane-Claire.

They just get back on the English assignment when the public address system sparks. "Will Lerue Stevens please come to Mrs. Barton's office. Lerue Stevens."

Jane-Claire startles, along with every other pair of eyes in the room. Everyone looks at Lerue. Mrs. Barton is the principal.

"Deep shit now." Someone calls from the back. Lerue gets a round of applause. People laugh. All except Jane-Claire.

Lerue rises from the table and raises his arms above his head like he's just won a prizefight. More applause, laughter. He turns and saunters from the library.

Jane-Claire pops up and runs to catch up with him.

Lerue looks down at her from over his shoulder. "What are you doing? Your name wasn't called."

"I'm your second." Jane-Claire won't let a member of the fellowship go into Mordor alone.

Class is in session, so the hall is deadly quiet. She worries as she jogs alongside Lerue. He stalks the hall to the principal's office.

"What happened? What'd you do?" Nothing like a sister pronouncing her brother guilty without a trial.

"It's got to be that damn math teacher," Lerue is livid.

Jane-Claire can tell by his face. If they were in the old west, he'd win the gunfight. He also would probably be an outlaw and die young. "They made a big mistake putting me in that class. I'm not about to do her stupid make up homework."

"Oh, I know what you mean. If that refugee counselor asks one more time if we're having suicidal thoughts, I might have to kill myself." Jane-Claire's statement is just one of those stupid comments she usually makes to relieve tension, but Lerue reacts.

He stops cold and grabs her shoulders. He bends down looks straight at her, eye to eye, which is fairly unusual since most of the time at school, he acts as if she's someone he met once.

"J.C., things aren't that bad. You'd tell me . . .." He can't say anymore. Then she understands what he's thinking.

Jane-Claire hugs him. "No. I'm only kidding. But that counselor's crazy, that's all she talks about."

Right about that time, a teacher pops her head from a classroom, "No PDAs in the hall."

"She's my sister." Lerue acts like Jane-Claire is a hot potato. He jumps away from her and highly offended, takes off down the hall.

Jane-Claire hurries after him and waves at the teacher, unsure if she believes him or not.

They wait in the reception area of Mrs. Barton's office for a full ten minutes. Lerue paces. Jane-Claire forces herself into a chair because the reception area is too small for two pacers. That does nothing to quell her steaming temper.

When Mrs. Barton opens the door and gestures them inside, she follows Lerue and stands slightly in back of him. Emma Barton is in her early forties and fairly tough looking. She greets Lerue with a big smile, which Jane-Claire counts as suspect.

Lerue frowns at Mrs. Barton.

Then Mrs. Barton looks past Lerue. "You must be Jane-Claire."

Who else? Jane-Claire thinks that but in reality, she just nods.

"I've heard so much about you. I'm glad you came down here with your brother." The principal continues with her "Bless Your Heart" act.

Every nerve in Jane-Claire's body strings tight and vibrates. She braces for bad news. Since the storm, it's easy to think the worst. She expects the world to drop out from under her at any moment. She plans on it. If she does that, maybe she won't be taken by surprise next time. Next time? Oh God, please no. Jane-Claire steps in front of Lerue and explodes.

"You're not treating Lerue right. He should be in Calculus BC or CD, MF, whatever. He should not be in that dippy do seminar class. He's way beyond that and you're boring the socks off of him with it. He needs a challenge. He deserves better math." Jane-Claire rapid fires her complaints to the principal in one long run on monologue.

Lerue stands appalled.

Mrs. Barton beams at him then offers her hand. "Congratulations, Lerue. This is the first time I've ever had a National Merit scholar dumped in my lap during his senior year. You're a special gift." She shakes Jane-Claire's hand as well. "And your sister is right. I've already made arrangements for you to go out to UAH for your math next semester if your family is still here."

Neither one of them know what to say but Jane-Claire does know what's going through her mind at that moment. She's an idiot but this is the beginning of the future. Loud and clear. This is good fortune, a break for the family, and they have Lerue to thank for it. This is the first time she can see a road ahead. Maybe the destruction of their lives as they knew it in Gulfport doesn't mean destruction for all time. Maybe one day, she won't think of the storm every second moment. One day it might become the past.

THAT EVENING, Jane-Claire helps serve at Kit's Supper Club. She's a little concerned that the dinner is scheduled on a school night. She has a lot of homework and other "get ready" stuff to do. She made the promise without checking first so she's stuck.

Another problem for her is that Kit and Martin did not invite her mom.

Kit prattles on about Supper Club exclusivity, how the group started years ago with four couples and how careful they are to keep the number of couples no greater than six. She emphasizes the word 'couples' as if Dona is an automatic DQ on that basis.

The Supper Club meets every month, sometimes every other month during the holiday season and winter. Hosting the dinner party rotates between the included couples. Why is Kit mentioning any of this unless she's doing something wrong by not asking her mom to attend?

Dona doesn't say a thing. At Kit's command, she stands at the kitchen counter cutting a brickbat hard loaf of stale Italian bread into cubes for fondue. She examines the bread carefully for mold.

Lerue, playing with Payton in the family room, opens his mouth, pretends to stick his finger in, and pantomimes retching. Payton who imitates anything Lerue does sticks his fingers in his mouth for real. Lerue yanks the toddler's fingers out super quick to keep him from throwing up.

Kit is queen of leftovers. She warms used food up ad nauseam and serves it until it's eaten. Her refrigerator is packed with packets of food that people might or might not have touched or tasted. The germ theory of contamination means nothing to her. Jane-Claire remembers the leftover pieces of picnic sandwiches that had baked in the late evening sun being served for weeks after the event.

Kit bustles through the kitchen. She counts wine bottles in several crates and fusses over trays of yucky cream cheesy looking appetizers and hors d'oeuvres.

Brittany and Jane-Claire stand nearby, careful to stay out of her way, but ready to help if possible. Brittany is nervous. She wants nothing more than to please Kit. Jane-Claire thinks that is an impossible goal.

"That's it! We're ready to roll." Kit heaves the crate of wine and kicks the side door open.

Jane-Claire hugs Dona and whispers, "Aren't these people your old friends?"

Dona shrugs. "We haven't seen too many of those lately."

Kit rushes back into the kitchen and directs Brittany and Jane-Claire to carry the extra appetizers and hors d'oeuvres from the member discount store. "Bring them to the car. And for God's sake, be careful."

"This bread is stale." Dona's comment arrests Kit in the doorway.

Kit considers the implications for a nanosecond then pipes, "Perfect for fondue."

Jane-Claire carries a tray and follows Kit into the garage.

Dona scrapes the stale bread from the cutting board into the garbage can as soon as Kit clears the kitchen. She looks at Lerue. "I think we need to celebrate your National Merit. Anybody for salad and pizza?"

Lerue cheers, and Payton cheers because of Lerue. This is the only happy moment this evening brings.

TONIGHT'S SUPPER Club will take place at a local physician's upscale house perched precariously on the side of Monte Sano, the big hill that overlooks Huntsville. Brittany and Jane-Claire struggle to transport the crates of wine and trays of food up a forty-five-degree angle driveway. Jane-Claire wonders how these people's kids ever learn to ride a bike or skate or even run. If they tried to play outside, they'd be at real risk of falling into a ravine or sliding down the drive into the street.

Inside the house, the kitchen appears brand new, which makes Jane-Claire think that no one ever cooks. As she watches the hostess, a tiny, battle ax tank of a woman, and Kit, she is sure that her assessment is on mark. They're not cooks at all, but they want to act like they are good cooks by having a fancy plated meal.

The main course is lamb, which is not an everyday meat that people usually cook. Kit and the hostess have no experience with it. They stab the poor thing with a thermometer every five minutes to check if it's done. That looks pretty nasty to Jane-Claire. A rack of lamb themometered to death.

The veggies don't look like much either. Nothing fancy, just green beans and mashed potatoes, but all the plates have to have the same number of beans and the same roundish mound of potato. Kit instructs Brittany and Jane-Claire on how to serve the plates so that they will all look the same on the table. On the first round of plates out, Brittany screws up and Kit consigns her to kitchen cleanup duty for the rest of the evening.

Jane-Claire calls on her ballet and acting skills. She can

mime anything, so she imagines that she is a butler who is secretly a pirate on a BBC series. Soon, she is invisible to the six fancy dressed couples surrounding the oval dining room table. She pours a ton of wine because she soon discovers that the real reason for the dinner is to drink different wines with each course. Every time a new course is served, she pours a different wine into a new glass. A white wine glass then a broader red wine glass and finally, a little crystal dinky glass, the kind that is pulled out of the back of a cabinet with glass windows. Brittany cleans more than fifty wine glasses that evening.

Jane-Claire serves small china plates of dessert: a store-bought pound cake with unripened strawberries. She pours the port into the dinky glasses.

She didn't know what to expect from the experience, but not this . . . This is why her mom wasn't invited.

"Are they going to move back?" The hostess tank announces open season when she asks the question. A chill tingles down her spine. She is one of the "they." She holds the partial bottle of port. The liquid quivers inside.

Kit scoffs, "She hasn't thought that far ahead. She hasn't thought at all."

"Refugees are taxing city resources. They're pouring in." Hostess's husband, the doc who claims to be the wine expert, snorts in disgust. "Such an influx."

"I heard one boy might steal a spot on the top 20 scholars list if he stays." A mother of a senior pipes up.

Jane-Claire clamps her mouth shut. Lerue should be the freaking valedictorian. From what she's seen so far, no one likes fresh competition.

Another man, a self-announced engineer on the arsenal, says, "Mark my words. This disaster's going to bankrupt the insurance companies. Our rates will be the ones to get hiked. We'll end up paying for the whole thing."

Martin interjects. Good old Martin. "Come on, guys. These are our neighbors the next state over. We're all Americans here."

Kit locks him down. "Oh, shut up Martin!"

Martin forces a smile and closes his mouth.

A petite woman, the only person who thanks Jane-Claire during her service that evening says, "Our church is thinking of sponsoring a dance for the school age refugees."

Jane-Claire considers labels and how often they're used just to keep someone out.

Kit jeers, "Would they even go?"

"No idea, and I don't care, but it would look great on my daughter's college resume if she organizes the effort." The man next to her thinks he has it all figured out.

Kit nudges the hostess with her elbow. "Her husband still works down there."

"Problems?" The hostess leans forward, anxious to hear the inside gossip. Everyone stops talking.

"Not real sure." At least Kit doesn't make up a bald-faced fallacy. They settle back in their chairs.

"I hear a lot of the hurricane kids are getting into drugs and alcohol." Mr. Engineer throws out his generalization.

Right. Jane-Claire wishes she had a glass right now. It would be okay since she's invisible. Her fury builds then she remembers a Bible verse out of the blue, "We are all as an unclean thing and all our righteousness are as dirty rags and we all do fade as a leaf and our iniquities like the wind have taken us away."

Jane-Claire doesn't need approval from these people and her mom doesn't need to eat dinner with them. She reaches for the swinging door into the kitchen but doesn't leave the room until the final salvo.

"I've never seen her so thin. She's on the hurricane diet." Kit is being so clever. Everyone laughs at Jane-Claire's mother.

Then Martin adds, "She's on the Kit diet."

Touché. Everyone but Kit roars.

THE DINNER ENDS LATE. Jane-Claire enters the guest room in Kit's house well after midnight. Her mom, exhausted, sleeps in her clothes on the bed. An uncomfortable mix of sympathy and rage flows through Jane-Claire.

Dona wakes in a start. "Oh, you're back. Sorry you had to stay out so late."

"Why should you be sorry?" Her mom is in no way responsible for the ridiculous Supper Club dinner running late. Everyone was too soused to get up and leave.

Dona senses trouble. "What happened? Did someone say something to you? Was someone rude?"

"Not to me." Jane-Claire shakes her head. The irony is too much to bear.

"Do you want me to get you something to drink? I'll stay up with you if you have homework." Dona sits up in bed, puzzled by her behavior. "Kit has a knack for saying the one thing she shouldn't. We all do that sometime. She just makes it a habit. Once when I was in college, I got food poisoning. I was really sick. High fever. Dehydrated. Kit brought me to the hospital, and she stayed with me till I was better. No one else came."

When Jane-Claire finally moves, she runs and hugs her mom. She holds onto her and never wants to let go. "I love you mom. I love you so much."

"You're my boon, J.C." Dona wraps her arms around Jane-Claire. "You're the best."

TWELVE

Nothing is Impossible

In the junior section of Parisian's at Parkway City Mall, Jane-Claire stands dead in the water.

Friday afternoon after a late night before at Supper Club is the worst possible time her mom can pick to take her shopping.

"Whoever heard of a teenage girl who doesn't want new clothes?" Her mom's smile is about to kill Jane-Claire as she trails after her through the crowded racks.

That comment doesn't begin to explain what bothers her right now. She had clothes and all kinds of other things.

Now, she owns two T-shirts, one from Dutch Mafia Coffee and a second with blue surf on the front that she bought on their family vacation in Oregon last summer. She took them the day of the storm because they were new.

Not anymore. Last summer seems like a lifetime ago.

Jane-Claire sleeps in a Tennessee Titans T-shirt that was a donation and the God-awful pajama pants because they are old and soft.

The Saturday before, Dona bought huge suitcases with plastic bottoms and expandable tops for herself, Lerue and Jane-Claire.

They don't want anchors. They want to be able to throw everything they own in the suitcase and go. If something happens again, travel light and leave nothing behind.

Jane-Claire drags her hand along the tops of the hanging clothes. She does not want to do this. She can't. She is tired and totally distressed. She mourns her loss and she is not ready to replace her past. Jane-Claire is not the least bit interested in looking at new clothes.

Dona holds a shirt in front of her. "Sweetheart, I can buy Lerue tan pants, a blue dress shirt, and he's set. Try something on, please."

"May I help?" A female voice asks the question.

Jane-Claire looks up and smiles in spite of herself. Mrs. Malbus is her stylish model of an interior design teacher. Teaching seems like a hobby for her, and she's head of the Home Ec department at the high school. Her classes cover interior and fashion design as well as basic cooking skills. Some of the students, based on how the classroom smells, desperately need to learn how to boil water. She is passionate about her work. She pays from her own pocket for all the magazines, fabrics, and food used in the course because she wants to have a great class. She is a definite bright spot at the high school.

"Mrs. Malbus. Mom, this is my interior design teacher." Jane-Claire introduces her to Dona.

"Rebecca." Dona and Mrs. Malbus hug each other.

Jane-Claire forgot that they knew each other in another time.

"Why don't you let me shop with Jane-Claire? I saw Lerue a few minutes ago wandering around the men's section like he's lost. Go over and help him. I'll be glad to give Jane-Claire a ride home when we finish." Mrs. Malbus is gracious with her time and interest.

Dona puts the request to Jane-Claire. "You okay with that?"

She surprises herself and nods. Dona gives Jane-Claire her credit card.

"Thanks, Rebecca." Dona seems relieved to exit the junior section.

Mrs. Malbus turns to Jane-Claire and critiques. "Now, with your coloring and style …"

Wow! A personal shopper. The burden of decision lifts then she remembers Natalie. School hasn't yet started back in Gulfport. She wonders if there are any stores left to buy clothes and Miss Shirin is always strapped for money.

Jane-Claire rubs the smooth plastic of her mom's credit card in her pocket. She and Nat are the same size.

"What about this, Jane-Claire?" Mrs. Malbus holds a couple of skirts and shirts together.

"Sure, whatever you say." Jane-Claire doesn't want to be the one to make the choice. Everything looks the same to her. She's not sure that she views color the same way anymore.

Somehow, she manages to buy a couple of dresses, a few shirts, and some jeans that Mrs. Malbus picks out for her. Jane-Claire will send some to Nat. Her teacher doesn't push and even takes the extra time to loop around on Garth Road when she drives her back to Kit and Martin's house on Chandler.

Garth Road borders an old family farm that is right in the middle of the city. The Appalachian foothills rise like fingers from level pasture land. Jane-Claire remembers riding on the back of a bicycle down to a Circle K gas station to get a Slurpee icee along this road when she was really little.

Since they evacuated, Lerue and Jane-Claire often circle this way before going back to the house. The air is always cooler, and they roll the windows down, even if the weather is hot out. As soon as they pass Randolph, the private school, there are only open fields and gentle hills. The wind washes tension away, and the drive is relaxing, restorative.

"Lerue and I come this way as much as we can. We call it the Garth Run. It reminds us of how we used to drive along Beach Highway. I just love it. It's like you're not even in the city." Jane-Claire rambles, happy to be talking about something nice with someone who treats her well.

Mrs. Malbus opens the windows and slows down a bit. "It's so beautiful . . . But I avoided Garth Road for many years."

"Why?" Jane-Claire straightens, shocked from her reverie. She's wary, like she's been drawn into a trap.

Mrs. Malbus keeps her eyes on the winding road. Her face is placid, too calm. "My husband and I were on Garth when he had his heart attack. He was driving and lost control of the car. It swerved. I was able to keep the car from crashing. I called 911 right away, but my husband died on this road."

Jane-Claire reacts. "Then why drive here?" She doesn't know anything about a husband except that Mrs. Malbus has a new one. Mom doesn't gossip, like other people in this town.

"How can you stand it? Why did you come here now?" Jane-Claire detects the self-protective edge creep into her voice.

"Don't worry. This isn't the first time I've been back. I drive the Garth Run all the time now. I agree with everything you said about it." Mrs. Malbus shrugs. "But I did avoid driving here for a long time. I somehow thought I'd betray my husband's memory by taking pleasure in the scenic beauty. Then I began to remember how much he loved life, right up to the time he passed. You don't betray your past by moving on with life. It takes time, Jane-Claire, but you can do it."

Mrs. Malbus doesn't say another thing, but Jane-Claire enjoys the rest of their ride together.

WHEN THEY ARRIVE at the Jones's house and pull into the circular drive, Jane-Claire doesn't see mom's Expedition, hard to miss, or Lerue's Passport. Mrs. Malbus asks her twice if she wants her to wait until mom and Lerue return but she's cavalier, so sure of herself, and insists no. She thanks her again for all her help. Jane-Claire appreciates that Mrs. Malbus did more than shop with her this afternoon.

She waves as she pulls off. But the minute Jane-Claire enters the house, she senses something is wrong. She should have turned around and waited outside on the steps. The upstairs rooms are already dark in the early autumn afternoon. Another week and they make the switch to daylight savings time. She roams through the main level, the guest bedroom, family room, kitchen, Kit's office. No one is here.

"Hey, anybody home?" Jane-Claire stands in the foyer. She is a stranger in the house, reluctant to sit down without permission. A noise grates from the basement. Hoping she didn't wake Payton or Brittany, she skips down the stairs.

"Brit? Payton? Hey." When Jane-Claire is almost to the bottom of the stairs, she stops short.

Randy sprawls in front of the television. "Game over. Dead," displays on the television screen. Her heart jumps to her throat. It thumps, beating hard in her chest. Can he hear it?

Randy is a wiry guy, a scrappy, unattractive definition of a creeper. The kind of person who always has the offset. He emanates the 'something wrong' vibe. He never pays attention to Payton or Brit. He acts like he landed a prize when he got Brittany pregnant because Kit and Martin are rich enough to support them. Randy is a manager at a McDonald's or some fast food restaurant. He's good with that because it gets him out of the house for a few hours, but he's even more happy to come back and take charity from his in-laws. Their home is a much nicer place than he could ever afford. He makes no attempt to move out. He has no intention of ever doing that.

"Hey, you looking for me?" He finishes the last of what looks to be a six pack of beer and pats his leg. Jane-Claire has visited that scene before.

"No." She laughs, tries to act nonchalant, and starts up the stairs before she can fully turn around. She trips and has to grab the bannister. "My mom will be home in a minute. She's right after me. Sorry to disturb you." Jane-Claire fights the urge to run but she should have taken off like lightening.

She climbs the stairs, only a little faster than normal, but the wiry dude is speedy.

He vaults over the recliner and runs like a flash to the stairs. Randy grabs her ankle from behind and yanks her foot out from under her.

Jane-Claire splats face down on the step's riser. She throws her arms in front but busts her lip on the wood.

Randy crawls over her like a spider. He pins her down and wraps his arms around and under her. He squeezes her breasts.

Jane-Claire gasps for air in pure panic and tries like

heck to scream, but the sound she makes is muted and minute. She tastes blood from her cut lip.

"Oh, is little girl scared?" He coos and nips at her. He sticks his tongue inside her ear.

Dumbass. That makes her mad. She twists to the side, pulls her knees up, and elbows Randy in the neck. He wheezes and curses at her.

She back kicks like a stupid donkey and breaks his grip. She scrambles up two stairs, then he's on top of her again. "Stay still little girl. Maybe I won't hurt you."

Like hell. She's already hurt. She squirms, bites, contorts, then he hits her. He punches her in the face so hard, she sees stars. She never thought she'd be caught so unaware and be so vulnerable like this. She never believed there was much of a difference between men and women. Girls are superheroes. Right? She's wrong. Men, even wiry slight ones, have a strength factor that's scary significant.

Jane-Claire's fingernails have always been long. Using her nails to defend herself will cost her. She's afraid, even more than in the hurricane, but she takes her chances and brings her fingernails to bear on his face. She scratches his arms, his hands like she's stuck in a coffin.

Fights on television and in movies seem sharp and clear, but in the middle of the action, it's all blurred melee. Randy clutches her arm and Jane-Claire is fully convinced; he's going to break it. She rotates into him to relieve some of the pressure. She rakes her nails across the side of his face. Someone growls. It's her.

Then a shadow flies over Jane-Claire. Randy lets go of her and falls back. He slides on his stomach to the bottom of the stairs.

Lerue lands two steps below Jane-Claire.

"What the hell are you doing?" He stands between Jane-Claire and Randy.

She melts into the stairs. Her hands shake. One finger bleeds where she ripped a nail.

Randy stands and swipes at his bloody cheek and hands. Jane-Claire nicked the corner of his eyelid. His face is a mess and he scowls at Lerue.

"Stay away from my sister." Lerue's so pumped, he can barely say the words. He rushes Randy and pushes him. Randy tumbles backwards and lands on top of the coffee table. The front legs of the table splinter into a million pieces.

Jane-Claire crawls up the stairs. Her lip bleeds. Her finger hurts. She's too afraid to cry.

"You think you know how to fight, boy?" Randy rolls to a stand, faces Lerue. "You just a stupid kid."

Lerue's taller, but Randy's meaner. He gives him a shit-eating grin and snaps a knife open.

Lerue throws his hands up and backs toward the stairs.

"Put that away!" Dona hurries and helps Jane-Claire to stand. She's never been so glad to see her. "Lerue, come here."

Lerue backs up the stairs. Randy starts to follow.

Dona shoves her hand in her purse hanging from her shoulder. As soon as Lerue is behind her, she steps down one stair. "Put that away. I have a gun in here and I know how to use it."

Randy eyes mom, cynical but hesitant. Jane-Claire mentally catalogues her mom's purse. She has a wallet, lipstick, wet wipes, Tylenol, pens, coupons, a cellphone but no gun. That's probably the only thing she doesn't have in her purse.

"Stand down. You think my husband would let me come up here unarmed?" Dona's voice is firm, sure.

That argument resonates with Randy. He closes the knife and watches as Lerue helps Jane-Claire back up the stairs. Dona is last to clear the staircase opening in the foyer.

"Get your things together." She doesn't have to say it twice.

The ordeal is over. Jane-Claire grabs her giant suitcase and has everything ready to go in less than three minutes. Lerue takes a little longer because he deflates the blow-up mattress he's been sleeping on in the living room and folds the linens. Good for him.

DONA INSISTS they wait for Kit and Martin to come home before they leave. They stand in the kitchen near the exit to the garage for almost an hour before they say good-bye to their hosts.

"I appreciate your hospitality, but two teenagers and me, as unsettled as I am, we've trespassed long enough." Dona doesn't specifically rat on Randy. Jane-Claire's swollen lip and bandaged finger tell the whole story.

Martin can't take his eyes from Jane-Claire as she stands holding an ice pack to her face. He paces and throws his hands up in exasperation, beside himself. "We try so hard to support their marriage for Payton's sake, but it's next to impossible. Brittany says she loves him. She lets him get away with anything."

Brittany stands nearby like a deaf mute. She holds Payton who whines and cries for Lerue. She refuses to go downstairs to talk with Randy who has been yelling for her from the basement since she got home. She's afraid. She should be.

Kit sits at her kitchen desk, avoids looking at her guests, and thumbs through random papers. When she does finally look at Dona, Jane-Claire can see her eyes glint.

"That son of a bitch should act like a man. He needs to buck up and support his family. He needs to get a real job."

"Kit, don't. Brittany made a mistake." Lerue and Jane-Claire stand beside Dona. The backpacks and new suitcases are already in the Expedition.

"I'm not paying for any damn divorce. She made her bed; she can lie in it." Kit points a finger at mom. "Like you. You should've listened to Mason. Taken those kids and gotten out of that house. You should have obeyed your husband."

"Yes, you're exactly right." Dona nods toward the door. "But I can only go from here."

Jane-Claire holds out a goody bag to Brittany. "We got makeup samples at school." Kit looks at her like the whole thing was her fault. Jane-Claire places the goody bag on Kit's desk and backs away.

Martin resorts to pleading. "Dona, you're a great influence on Brit. She listens to you and Payton loves playing with the kids. What about Payton? At least stay until Mason has things figured out."

That is the exact wrong thing to say. Dona faces Martin. Her eyes narrow. "No, this is my decision."

"Y'all have been through so much. Kit say something." Martin places his hands on Dona's shoulders. She shakes him off.

Kit picks up a letter opener and tears open the top of an unopened envelope. "We have to respect Dona's wishes. It's not like she's moving back to the coast. They can visit anytime."

"I'm sorry, Martin. Think of your daughter and your little grandson. Think of them. Thank you again for your kindness to my family. Thank you." Dona exits. Jane-Claire and Lerue follow her from the house.

THIRTEEN

Wal-Mart or Mercedes

After the *Lord of the Flies* episode, the journey mirrors *Lord of the Rings* as Dona, Jane-Claire, and Lerue travel from one devastated area to another trying to maneuver their way through tremendous obstacles.

People should be helpful but often are not. Who is genuine? Look again. Who can be trusted? They parallel the quest and inch forward. They persevere. The trek lies before them, but the way is unknown.

The night they leave the Jones's house, they sleep in the car because other refugees are living in hotel rooms in the city. No Vacancy.

The next morning, Dona rents a furnished apartment off Airport Road, near the Parkway City Mall and just over the railroad tracks. The apartment has three bedrooms, two baths and is on the second story of a four-apartment brick building surrounded by shade trees. The location is pretty close to the dance studio and not too far from school.

Because the apartment is furnished, Dona doesn't have to go out and buy mattresses, television sets. . .. too numerous to list. The manager outfitted the apartment with furniture, sheets, towels, basic cookware and calls it a refugee special. Dona just walks in with the backpacks and ready to go. Perfect.

But Dona doesn't think so.

Walking into that apartment is a low point for her. Possibly a point of no return. She signs the shortest lease she can then enters the apartment alone through the back door from an enclosed rear staircase.

Shouldering all three backpacks, Dona walks into a kitchen that has four walls and no windows.

On the stained Formica counter, a welcome basket from a Christian Church group greets her. The basket contains napkins, laundry detergent, paper plates, and a can opener.

She picks the can opener up, turns it over in her hand, then puts it back in the basket. What a symbol of all the little minutia items that must be replaced.

She follows the circular pattern of the apartment and continues from the kitchen to a dining room furnished with a square game table and four rolling chairs.

Next is the living room then around to a hallway where there is a laundry closet. The master bedroom and bath at the front of the apartment faces the street.

Two smaller bedrooms sharing a Jack and Jill bathroom are located at the back of the building and look out on the alley which will serve as parking for their SUVs.

Dona chooses the bedroom just off the kitchen.

The furniture is made of plastic. She opens the closet and the chest of drawers. There's nothing in them, and nothing to put in them. She drops the backpacks on the bed and sits down. Her face is blank, set expressionless. Tears well in her eyes.

Then Lerue and Jane-Claire arrive from school. They burst through the kitchen entrance door.

Dona stands, checks her hair, wipes her tears. She smooths her clothes and greets them.

"Hey, I'm in here." Her voice is clear, cheerful. She never tells anyone how she first felt about the place till much later.

Lerue and Jane-Claire enter the bedroom like two children who just came downstairs on Christmas morning.

"Can I take the master?" Lerue's eyes beg.

Dona smiles, "Sure, I was going to suggest it."

"Mom, this is totally awesome." Lerue pulls a triumphant fist to his chest. He grabs his backpack from the bed and hurries to stake his claim.

Lerue and Jane-Claire love the apartment. They think it's wonderful. There's a big red suede couch in the living room that looks totally ridiculous, and a grandma chair covered in off white, maybe the fabric is just dirty, velvet.

Lerue sits and spins in the grandma chair with magic qualities that relieve stress.

The setup is great. They eat on the couch and use the coffee table as their dinner table. They alternate watching *Lord of the Rings* and *Harry Potter* on a big tube style television every night. The square game table in the little dining room is reserved as a desk for homework.

Jane-Claire takes the middle bedroom, sandwiched between Lerue and her mom.

Every night as they sleep, she can always tell when someone rolls over or changes position because the plastic covering on the mattresses and box springs makes a crinkle noise.

That's okay, she knows they're close.

At home in Gulfport, Dona had a rule that if a poster was hung on the wall, it had to be framed. Because of the frame size, Jane-Claire could only fit one poster in her bedroom on Second Street. But at the apartment, she eventually puts up movie posters over every square inch of wall space.

In her mom's bedroom, someone left a little dinky television, Jane-Claire guesses the previous person who lived there.

The television is so old it can't even get cable, only three channels. Dona confirms that was the norm when she was a kid. But there is one channel that plays old movies, so Jane-Claire and her mom often hang out in the little bedroom. Since the bedroom is right off the kitchen, they lounge on the bed while Dona cooks, waits for water to boil or whatever.

The little television is so old Jane-Claire expects it to be only black and white, but the ancient little box is color. She considers it as a gift.

The apartment becomes a safe house where they live a day to day life again. Between Mom, Lerue, and Jane-Claire, conversation quickens. They switch from one topic to the next and are always able to follow the flow and know what they're talking about.

Everyone gets along well, and they never bring up the storm anymore, unless they need to. Conversations focus on school, sports, dance, and what's happening now, as in today.

Everything is pretty okay, except Saturday afternoons. Saturday afternoons are Lerue's bane. He's busy with homework, new friends, and sports the rest of the week. Jane-Claire is at ballet almost every weekday evening till seven and on Saturdays till noon. Dona subs and guest teaches at the ballet school some evenings, but nothing happens on a Saturday afternoon.

Huntsville tends to be gray then, as if it is a twilight

world. Neither hot nor cold. The rising foothills surrounding the city shade out bright colors and sunshine.

Dona and Jane-Claire become wary on Saturday afternoons. They make hot dogs and chili for lunch. They look for matinee movies that start around three and end two hours later in time for dinner. Every once and awhile, they come up short. When they do, the guilt and horror of their recent experience is ready to pounce.

Lerue wants to be in Gulfport. He wants to be helping Dad rebuild the house.

No one agrees that this is what he should be doing, but on Saturday afternoons Lerue is a fervent believer.

He falls apart.

Dona and Jane-Claire know that it's never a good thing when he watches *Gladiator*. That movie gets him crying. Then he starts railing and yelling about going home and being a Gulfport Admiral not a Huntsville Panther. He goes on and on about how much Dad needs him, which he does but during this time, still so close to the storm, very little rebuilding is going on.

Gulfport is in the throes of clearing debris and assessing damage. Building materials are scarce and cost many times more than they are worth. Price gouging is rampant, and workers are nonexistent.

Facts don't stop Lerue. His guilt, and even shame, at not being in Gulfport to help Dad boil over like a pot of pasta.

Dona wishes she could pick him up and hold him. She would pat his back and rock him if she could, but he's too big for that. He won't accept touch or smoothing.

Dona and Jane-Claire try to stay out of his way for a while and let the steam blow.

Then Dona appeals to his stomach.

There is a distinct German flavor to Huntsville, introduced and encouraged by the rocket scientists that moved there from Germany after World War II. Ole Heidelberg is a restaurant where Germany prevails, and Lerue loves to go there.

On Saturdays that are wash outs, Dona always suggests going there for dinner. She starts by saying that she's wondering what the Riesling of the month is, and she asks Lerue if he would mind driving back because she would enjoy a glass of wine. She would enjoy quite a bit more than a single glass, but Dona is disciplined if nothing else.

Lerue loves to drive the Expedition wreck because it makes him feel like he's *Mad Max*. Somehow, he pulls himself together, and off they go.

During a dinner of wiener schnitzel and roulades with plenty of brown bread and real butter, the conversation always turns into a debate about Wal-Mart or Mercedes.

What does that mean?

When a person has to replace everything in their life from underwear to yes, can openers, they have a chance to analyze where to spend the money.

Is it better to buy the cheapest quality and use it till it breaks then replace it?

Or is it better to invest in the best quality and hope that insures lasting for the long haul?

Dona, Jane-Claire, and Lerue have this conversation with some frequency, and they always reach a compromise balance point.

Some things should be disposable and bought from Wal-Mart, and some things should be the Mercedes quality. Don't worry. They will continue the conversation on the next downtrodden Saturday.

The threesome is grateful beyond words for the refugee

special. The apartment fosters stability which allows some healing. They can rest, sleep, forget. . . Then Mason comes for a visit.

FOURTEEN

Looters and Thieves

Mason's first visit to his family since the evacuation to Huntsville is to attend the high school's annual breakfast in honor of their National Merit Finalists.

Lerue counts as a Huntsville High achievement now.

Dona, Jane-Claire, and Lerue brace for Mason as if another named storm is barreling over them.

There will be plenty of hurricane talk and the family will struggle to have a regular conversation with Mason about school, college plans, and Huntsville itself.

True dat!

All Mason wants to talk about is the hurricane, the house on Second Street, and his work. He doesn't follow them when they try to switch topics. He loses his place and keeps asking them to repeat and retread.

Everyone presses each other's buttons very quickly because they are so off topic.

The family is misaligned. Mason is not part of their normal day anymore. He's been dealing with the 'in your face' aftermath. They are dealing with the reestablishing day to day basics of recovery.

The two perspectives don't mesh and the big bone of contention is the apartment.

Though it has been a lifesaver to Dona, Jane-Claire and Lerue, the apartment only signifies added, unnecessary expense to Mason.

Jane-Claire gets to the Huntsville High library early that morning to help Mrs. Malbus and Mrs. Quintero set up for the event. To tell the truth, she is relieved to get out of the apartment.

She hopes she meets her dad again, because the man who just walked into the room with her mom isn't him.

That man wears steel toed boots like he's still walking the debris field. They remind Jane-Claire of the Guidos' beloved Jesuit school uniforms. He scowls at everyone in the room. He hates them because they don't share his pain and distress. That man is offended by the normalcy. Jane-Claire understands that it hurts.

No one likes to see life dismiss another's tragedy and go on without them, but it does.

Lerue looks awesome with his National Merit Scholar medallion hanging from his neck. He poses for pictures with other National Merit seniors. He talks and laughs with other students. Well done.

Jane-Claire had been worried about him, but now she believes the fact that he is a senior works in his favor. Next year will be new and completely different, so he can practice, even enjoy this year because of the limited scope.

"I'm so glad you could get off to attend," Dona tries to engage Mason in the present. "I'm so proud of Lerue. Finishing those applications won't be easy, but we're working on it."

Mason stands stiff, irritated. He scans the assembly and judges them harshly. "You and the kids seem to be doing alright."

Dona grimaces. "As well as we can."

"I feel like I'm on furlough from the trenches." Here he goes. He can't let go of the disaster. Not for a minute.

"What's wrong, did something happen?" All she can do is listen. She can't change a thing.

"Looters stole the hot tub the other night." Mason drops well placed bombs at inopportune times.

Disturbed, Dona's face creases. "Oh, Mason, I'm so sorry. Did you call the police?"

"There's nobody around to look into stuff like that. The police only investigate murders." Mason is so mentally exhausted that his speech is slurred, disconnected.

"The neighborhood's a wasteland. I'm beginning to think that won't change in our lifetime."

Dona takes Mason's elbow and leads him to a nearby table. She helps him sit down as if he's a recovering invalid.

"Let me get you some coffee, something to eat."

Dona walks to Jane-Claire in the buffet line.

Jane-Claire fixes her eyes past her mom's shoulder and squarely on her dad as if she has to watch him like an unruly child or a crazy person who might explode at any moment. "Why did he even come here if he's going to act like this? Nothing we do is right. He's just bossing us around."

Dona shakes her head and shuts her daughter down. "Jane-Claire, Dad's tired. He has been on the front line. You know how devastating that is."

Jane-Claire sighs and nods. She does know, and she wonders if she's just playing pretend here. Hide the truth. Don't let anyone know how bad things are.

Is that all they've been doing? Trying to act better than they feel? Fake it till they make it? Has she just become a really good liar? She calls it a balance. Dwelling on disaster prevents living.

Dona brings some food and a coffee to Mason.

Jane-Claire can hear them over the short distance.

"Any news about a trailer?" Dona fixes the coffee for Mason.

"I spent hours in line and on the phone." Mason complains. He has no idea how many hours Dona has been on the phone. She doesn't say anything because it would only start a fight.

"Looters trapped Dr. Well's wife in their trailer last week." Mason's voice is flat.

"How did he get a trailer?" Dona asks the obvious.

"Wells ran from the emergency department with his gun. When he showed up, the looters hightailed it out of there." Mason doesn't address her question but goes on with his story. He looks far away, pensive.

"We can talk later." Dona smiles at Lerue who waves.

"I'm glad somebody's happy." Mason sounds resentful. He was National Merit too.

"This is Lerue's day, Mason. Be happy for him." Dona is radiant and perfectly false.

Jane-Claire's heart is so heavy that she can hardly stand up straight. She tries to smile and slaps the eggs onto the foam plates. Are we having fun yet?

"Gently now." Mrs. Malbus catches Jane-Claire's shoulders and gives her a little hug. "We're all in this together." Jane-Claire's tension eases.

"Lerue could have been killed, and it would have been your fault." Mason sneers at Dona.

"He wasn't." Dona and Mason sit together and look anywhere but at each other.

"I was so glad when those FEMA docs showed up, but they don't see many patients. They don't work nights."

This is Mason's way of changing the subject, only he really doesn't. He just wallows further in the hurricane swamp.

Jane-Claire imagines that she's playing butler at Kit's Supper Club as she offers a plate to a proud grandmother.

"At least somebody came. At least they're doing something." Dona tries to spin Mason's perception of the situation.

"They take the easy cases. What they're doing is stealing business away from the docs who stayed and are trying to rebuild their practices." Mason's anger seethes.

Nothing's fair. Jane-Claire chants this to herself over and over. For the first time, she finds herself thinking "Things could be worse." Her stomach flips a couple of times.

"What about our family? What about us, Mason?" Dona tries to turn the conversation.

Mason won't buy it. "The hospital's closing temporary housing. They took the laundry out. First Baptist gives out packs of new underwear on Sundays." He drones as if delivering a news report.

Jane-Claire stands in the serving line and with a great deal of effort, slides scrambled eggs onto the plates with a pasted on smile.

She ponders what can be done to help her dad. How can she break him out of this? How do people come home after war? Or after being in a concentration camp? Or any other bad thing? How do they live again?

"Fresh underwear must be a total draw for the congregation." Dona tries to make a little funny. Epic fail. "Where are you going to sleep when the hospital closes its quarters?"

"I'll keep working to get a trailer or rent some dog of an apartment. But two apartments? Two electric bills, plus our mortgage, which has to be paid, even if the house is uninhabitable. I feel like we're drowning in debt." Mason pushes himself further under.

"At least we did have the flood insurance. Remember, the lawyer laughed when we bought it." Mason doesn't react so that piece of alright doesn't mean anything. "Any news on rebuilding?"

Mason snorts, disgusted. "I can't even get anyone to meet with me."

"I've heard people are in town looking for investment property." Dona keeps in touch with her old neighbors. They've stayed close to commiserate and share news.

"Yep, the vultures are circling." Her implication suddenly hits him. Mason turns and actually looks Dona in the eye. "Wait, you're telling me you want to sell?"

Mason's voice is too strident. People look.

Dona leans closer, lowers her voice. "We might consider relocating. At least until Jane-Claire graduates."

"I can't believe you just said that." Mason looks like he wants to hit Dona.

"You say Gulfport's as lawless as a wild west town." Dona hands him a direct quote.

"It's true. We've seen over fifty rape cases this month, compared with five in all of last year. What would you call it?" Mason riles.

Dona pats his arm. "A problem. A big one. J.C.'s 15 years old." She looks toward Jane-Claire. "She's been such a blessing. Both of them have been so brave. "

Mason leans into his wife. "I bought a gun, Dona."

Jane-Claire overhears her dad's pronouncement and plops a whole serving of scrambled eggs onto the floor in response. She doesn't make one move to pick them up. She can't. She waits for her mom's reaction.

Dona's eyes pop. "Mason, we don't own guns."

"I was the only doc in the room that didn't have one. I even got a conceal permit." Mason is finally animated.

Jane-Claire stoops to clean up her mess. There's serious subtext going on here.

"You always hated the thought of shooting someone and then having to treat them. You said it defeated the purpose of being a doc." Dona is hurt, confused.

Jane-Claire remembers that her dad never let Lerue go hunting even though most guys in Mississippi as a rule skip school the opening day of any hunting season.

"I carry it all the time now." Mason states the fact with no emotion.

Jane-Claire bolts upright. That was no subtext at all.

Dona gawks, mouth open. She looks around. "You have it here? At the school?"

Holding a camera, sweet, smiling Mrs. Quintero, brings Lerue to Mason and Dona's table. She motions Jane-Claire over. "Come on, let me get a family picture of y'all."

Dona stands and places her hand on Mason's shoulders. He doesn't move.

Lerue and Jane-Claire gather around him for the photo, one of the best the family ever takes together. All smiles and perfectly balanced, they never betray how at odds they are at that moment.

BACK AT THE APARTMENT, Dona is fighting mad as she stalks into the kitchen ahead of everyone.

"Did you put it in the car?" She pitches her purse into a far corner of the kitchen counter.

"Yes." Mason paces the tight space.

Lerue and Jane-Claire carry boxes in from dad's car. He brought them from Gulfport. Although the boxes are new, Jane-Claire can smell the dust and dirt from debris inside.

"Why couldn't you have just stayed with Kit and Martin? That's what I wanted. This apartment is an extra twelve hundred dollars a month, not counting cable and utilities." Mason berates Dona. He's on a tear.

"I'll tell you why." Jane-Claire pipes up. One look from her mom tells her to keep her mouth buttoned.

"We couldn't. Take my word for it." Dona is in full battle gear.

The heat of their anger mixed with the Gulfport dust is enough to make Jane-Claire gag.

"You don't understand, dad. It just wasn't possible." Lerue stacks the boxes on the table.

Mason nods. "Thanks, I have more in the trunk." He tosses his keys to Lerue.

"Okay," Lerue sounds doubtful. Jane-Claire follows her brother as he exits, but she stands in the doorway and delays going down the stairs.

"What's in the boxes?" Dona moves Lerue's college applications from the table. She consolidates the papers and places them on top of the refrigerator.

"Some of your books. Tasha Tudor. Golden Books. CDs. DVDs I recovered. Our wedding silver. Salt water stripped the finish off but maybe we can have it redone. I found a few pictures." Mason catalogs the past.

"What am I supposed to do? What? Everything's ruined." Dona recoils as she smells the stench rising from the boxes.

"You could try to salvage something. It can be done." Mason acts as if Dona walked out and left all of their treasures behind without a care.

Jane-Claire wants to scream at him. 'We were there. We saw what happened. Why are you doing this to us?'

"You brought me corpses, Mason." Dona only says the truth.

Mason doesn't want to hear it. "Calm down. I thought it might remind you of home. Is anything else wrong?" He diverts her attention because she's right. He thought all this stuff would make a difference if he boxed it up and brought it to her, but it means nothing.

"Isn't this enough?" Dona stands her ground.

Mason pulls his work card. "You should see what I've been dealing with at the hospital."

Dona throws her arms up. Surrender. Nothing ever compares with the ER is a given fact of their family. Go for the pressure. That's where the stakes are greatest. Life and death. Stakes don't get higher than that.

Jane-Claire watches her parents bleed all over the floor. In her mind, she begs them to just hug each other. Please. Just to love each other.

"That's not what I mean. Listen, I'm meeting Lori's brother." Mason tries to move the subject back to the house.

Jane-Claire stands there and prays. 'Back off. Don't do this. Stop. Don't say anymore.'

"Lori?" Dona eyes Mason as she shoves the boxes in a corner.

"One of the nurses. Her brother's a decent contractor, an honest guy."

"The house is not important anymore." Dona reaches the ultimate conclusion.

"Dona, it's our home. We can't give up on it. That's where we're going to retire. Remember our plan? We'll have the house by the beach, so everyone will want to visit." Mason holds his hands out. He's pleading now.

Dona shakes her head, goes to Mason, and takes hold of his arms.

"No, not any more. Our home is wherever our family is. It's not a place. It's only us. We could rebuild, only to be destroyed by another storm. Could you handle that? I can't."

Then Lerue bounds up the stairs, past Jane-Claire, and into the kitchen with an oval shaped red canvas bag. "Wow, Dad found my skimboard."

The case reeks of bleach and detergent.

Lerue lifts the skimboard over his head and almost hits the ceiling light. Hoots and hollers. That's how he avoids crying.

"Gee, Dad, you fixed it. I didn't know you could work fiberglass." Lerue unzips the case and points to a neat, sanded fiberglass patch on one edge.

Mason acts indignant as if his own son doesn't know a damn thing about him.

Jane-Claire watches her family disintegrate, concerned for them all.

"Dad owned a sailboat in medical school. He used to take me out on Lake Pontchartrain." Dona looks at Mason. "Thank you. It was really nice of you to fix it for Lerue." Strained silence follows. Dona looks away as she remembers better days.

Lerue puts the skimboard on top of the boxes and runs to his room. He reappears moments later in a board bathing suit.

Dona startles. "Whoa, no beaches here. Only college applications. The deadline…"

Lerue's face twists and he pounds his hand on the tabletop. "I'm going over to the field by the old airport. I'm going to skim."

"No. Scholarship deadline is tomorrow." Dona gets in Lerue's face, but the top of her head comes up to his armpit, so this doesn't really have the effect she's aiming for.

"Who cares?" Lerue heads for the door.

"Mason." Dona passes Lerue off to his dad.

Jane-Claire is surprised but her dad does step up to the challenge. "Your mother says no."

"What the. . ." Mason wrests the skimboard from Lerue in one smooth move. "Don't ever say that. I knew a kid. He had Down's Syndrome and that was the only word he ever learned. He was so happy, he said it all the time, till nobody could take him anywhere. Not to church, school. That one word ruined his life."

Lerue backs from Mason and goes after Dona. "Why'd you leave, Dad, why? We should all be together. We should be down there helping."

"Wait a minute," Dona prickles. "I know this may sound old fashioned, maybe even stupid, but I made a big mistake not evacuating to the hospital."

"Thank God, it wasn't fatal, but I do regret it. In coming to this town, I obeyed my husband. This is what he wanted me to do." She points at Mason who stands convicted.

"Mom's right. This whole thing was my idea. I stayed behind to work and support my family. I miss you all, and I love you more than you know."

They stay. No one is willing to make a move. Jane-Claire wishes she could disappear but instead she turns to Lerue and blurts, "Lerue, don't be such a dick."

Mason laughs. "Like father, like son."

And the tension dissipates. Dona calms. Lerue backs off.

"Ah, okay. I'll grill the hamburgers." Lerue pulls the platter of raw burgers from the fridge. Jane-Claire follows him out of the apartment and down the steps to the grill near the parking lot.

WHILE LERUE LIGHTS the gas barbecue grill cemented near the apartment exit door, Jane-Claire tries to convince herself that everything's going to be okay.

She piles excuses up, one on top the other, like a house of cards. Everyone is tired. They're just tense and nervous about dad's visit. In the end, love will prevail. They are family. Love will save the day.

Jane-Claire is never far from the free floating fear she experienced during the hurricane and right after. What happens next? Where will they live? What will they do? But storm or no, does anyone ever really know?

Her answer is no, people just think they do.

A brisk wind from the hills surrounding the city signals the change of seasons. Autumn in Gulfport is anticlimactic. Leaves eventually turn brown sometime in January and fall off but here, the leaves are bright, colorful, and rain down like tears. She tilts her head back and look up at the leaves showering all around her.

Is the present all they really have? Today? Just this single moment?

Lerue slaps the hamburger on the grill. The meat sizzles and smells so good. "Should we tell dad?"

Jane-Claire pulls from her reverie. "What?"

"About Randy. What do you think? Was I really being a dick just 'cos I wanted to skim? I miss it." Lerue keeps an eye out for flare ups.

"No, you weren't. Not really. I had to say something that might stop them." Jane-Claire walks next to Lerue.

"Mom and Dad are going in circles. Dad's hellbent on rebuilding the house, the past, and Mom only sees the future." Lerue seems intent on grilling, but he's really analyzing.

"It's like *Lord of the Rings*." Jane-Claire backs up a step, raises her arms above her head and turns in a circle to dance with the leaves.

"Everything's like *Lord of the Rings* with you." Lerue laughs and flips the burgers.

She stops and looks at her so serious sweet brother. "Well, because it is. Samwise said it. 'By rights, we shouldn't be here, but here we are, and we just have to keep going.'" Jane-Claire wants to add that it's easier to talk in stories because reality hurts. Stories soften the blow. "Great stories. The ones that really matter. . ."

Lerue smiles, then brushes leaves from the grill. "If people price gouge granola bars, then building materials must be out of sight. How are we going to pay for redoing the house?" He's kept a running discussion going with dad all day about the logistics of rebuilding, or at least making one room habitable.

Lerue suddenly stops. "Wait. Dad's not looking in the right place. Think about it. All the better houses and apartments were on the Gulf side of the railroad tracks. He needs to check out the other side."

Just then, Mason exits the apartment. He's in a hurry and Dona is at his heels. He waves to Lerue and Jane-Claire. "Sorry, I have to get going."

Dona grabs at Mason's shoulder. "Please wait, at least have something to eat."

"I need to leave. I don't want to be driving too much in the dark." Mason looks as if he's escaping an apartment fire.

"The hamburgers will be ready in a few minutes." Lerue is hurt but doesn't want to take sides against him. "Dad, you need to look for a place in the old neighborhood. Just a studio apartment. Ask Ed. He'll know. He'll help you."

Jane-Claire trembles. Crushed, she can't stand this. Why does he have to leave so soon?

Mason walks to Jane-Claire. He kisses her hair, hugs her, and pushes her away at the same time. She doesn't reciprocate.

He grabs her chin and tries to make her look in his eyes. "Wish we could have our bonfire. Some parts of the beach reopen this weekend."

"You can't even have a hamburger?" Jane-Claire doesn't mean to, but that pushes a button she didn't even know existed.

Mason flares, defensive and doctor like. "At least I didn't pull a Shirin. She flat abandoned Nat. Left her with that ancient grandmother woman who doesn't even seem to like her. She just took off."

Jane-Claire is stricken. "What? When did this happen?"

Mason laughs, a little "ha, I gotcha" moment. Like he relishes any victory. "The day of the hurricane." He says it plain, ungarnished.

"Why didn't you tell me before? Nat's my friend. I've been really worried about her. I mail letters to the hospital and her house that's not even there anymore. I haven't gotten anything from her. Not a word. I didn't know." Jane-Claire is furious. Her nostrils widen in anger.

"I've checked on her." Mason shrugs. "Her arm will be alright, but Shirin didn't help a damn thing by leaving." He backs away, avoids a cool Dona, and shakes Lerue's hand. "I've got to get going."

"Sure, you do." Jane-Claire runs between Mason and his beloved truck that somehow didn't get a scratch in the storm. Her hands ball into fists. "No matter what's falling apart with us, you're always on your way out. You've got to go to work."

Mason hesitates. Dona stands silent. Lerue covers his face and turns away.

"Go on. Get out. Go. Did you add anything to today? I don't think so." Jane-Claire snarls at her dad, and it's all she can do not to kick him. She didn't think she'd be the one to draw blood that day but such as it is.

"I'm sorry." Mason whispers his apology to the cement. He leans forward to kiss Jane-Claire.

She backs away.

He looks at his family then hurries to his truck, gets in, and drives off.

The hamburgers char in the flames from the grill. The burgers are ruined.

Lerue moves the blackened circles to the outer edges of the grill but concedes that it's too late. "Man, who's the dick now?"

Jane-Claire spins around and shouts to her mom and brother. "Is he a doc or a father?"

"A doc." Dona and Lerue answer in unison.

Dona shakes her head. "J.C., not everyone in the world is always going to think you're the next best thing to sliced bread. Sometimes you can't just fix things because you want to." She throws her hands in the air as she retreats to the apartment.

Lerue turns the gas grill off and pitches the ruined burgers, one by one, into the dumpster across the street. His aim is pretty good. He only misses once.

Jane-Claire plops to the curb and buries her face in her hands. "It's not fair." Her voice is raspy, broken. "It's just not fair."

"Nope." Lerue runs across the street, retrieves the

nothing burger from the asphalt and throws it over his shoulder into the dumpster.

He runs back to sit down beside her. "I keep a mental inventory of what I had that stays intact until I go to use something, and it's not there. Then I realize it's gone, and that's when I miss it."

"What?" Jane-Claire raises her head. Her face is splotchy, and her mouth hangs open.

Lerue sits beside Jane-Claire on the curb. "That violin in your closet bothers me. It's not part of our inventory, and the way you have it standing next to your camera. They look like grave markers to me."

Jane-Claire doesn't want to hear this. She buries her head and covers her ears. "I'm keeping it for Nat. It was her idea. And I just can't film anything right now." She yells her answer into her knees.

"When I saw that storm coming, I knew we were done. I calculated wind speed, trajectory, the weight and force of water. There was no way. It would have been safer to go to the hospital, but I didn't want to miss it. And that's why I wanted to go skim so bad. I knew it would be the last time. What happened wasn't a surprise. I expected as much." Lerue pats his sister's back. "Try not to lose things that are impossible to lose."

FIFTEEN

Makeshift Morgue

Dona is up early the next morning, but Jane-Claire is up earlier.

From her bedroom, she can hear her mom sorting through the debris scarred paraphernalia that dad dumped into the middle of her clean kitchen yesterday, and her cough as she breathes the dust of moldy children's books. The CDs clatter as she washes them in the sink.

Jane-Claire looks at the violin case propped in the corner of the almost empty closet. Her video camera in the gadget bag sits next to it.

She wonders if the thoughts she woke with this morning are leftover dreams or predictive visions. Guess she'll have to find out. She can't think about her plan too much.

She just has to do it. If there was any other way. . ..

Lerue buzzes into Jane-Claire's room. "Time to go. I'm ready when you are."

Jane-Claire is taking him out to breakfast at Gibson's, the good ole boy's barbecue restaurant on the Parkway, to discuss the details.

She nods and hands Lerue the violin. He stuffs the case in his swim gear duffle. She crams the gadget bag with her video camera into her backpack.

They walk through the kitchen on their way out.

"Later gator." Lerue waves to the air and slips through to the back staircase.

"Bye, mom. Love you." Jane-Claire pastes on a smile, blows a kiss, and prays that her mom knows how much she means what she says.

"Y'all are up early." Dona surfaces from the chaos. "I'll fix some breakfast if you want?"

"We're going to Gibson's." Lerue yells from halfway down the back stairwell.

"I'll have it all cleaned up by this afternoon." Dona smiles, but her heart is broken. How could Mason do this to her?

Jane-Claire almost wants to abandon her plan and stay home to help her.

"Let's go." Lerue's voice booms from the bottom outside door.

"You okay, J.C.?" Dona's eyebrows furrow.

"Yeah, I'm good." Jane-Claire never knew a lie could roll off her tongue quite so easily. "Hang Tough." She rushes from the apartment, relieved to get out without bursting into tears. Dona should have guessed. Jane-Claire didn't say anything about seeing her this afternoon.

Dona gazes at the upheaval surrounding her. Hurricane Mason hit. He brought the storm with him. She can't blame the kids for abandoning ship, but she wishes they would have invited her to join them. She has a full day of work ahead.

After placing the washed CDs on paper towels to dry, she grabs a broom and sweeps the moldy dust into a pile. She moistens paper towels and kneels to wipe the fine dirt up from the floor. The entire apartment will have to be cleaned to keep the smell of the debris and the black mold spores from infiltrating. No one can deal with the contamination. No one wants to.

Her precious books are ruined, spoiled by salt water then left closed to dry. She wears gloves to lift them from the box Mason packed them in and shoves them directly into the garbage can.

She stomps on the empty box to break it down then stuffs the flattened cardboard into the garbage bag with the books. She does all this before realizing that she should have just thrown the whole box undisturbed into the dumpster.

Maybe she wants to identify the dead.

See them one last time.

Dona spends the entire morning corralling mold and rotted dirt. When her cellphone rings, she welcomes the distraction but answers without any idea who could be calling. Insurance adjusters never initiate calls.

"Hello?"

"I just got notice from the high school. Seems your boy's not in class today. I bet that little shit's halfway back to the coast. What the hell does he think he's doing?" Kit barks over the phone.

Dona is not in the mood to take anything else. She's been primed by the morning of burial duty. She listens to Kit and even waits for her to completely finish before taking a deep breath and ripping her reply.

"Don't you ever call my son a little shit. Maybe if you'd been kinder to your own daughter, if Brittany believed you really loved her, she'd think more of herself than to hook up with that redneck hick."

Dona hyperventilates, and her hands shake as she closes the call, but she only said what she believes. The broom falls from her hands and the handle rattles as it hits the floor.

She strips the gloves off, and doesn't even bother to wash her hands, but grabs her purse, car keys and is out of the door in one fluid motion worthy of choreography in a ballet.

DONA DRIVES her wrecked Expedition down Whitesburg at the top side of the speed limit and makes a left turn on a yellow light onto Marsheutz.

She pulls in front of the high school and dives into the parking place reserved for the principal.

She exits the car and sprints up two flights of stairs to the front entrance of the school in the ninety-degree Indian summer heat.

Dona catches the rail at the top of the stairs and stops for a moment to catch her breath. That is a lost cause. She charges through the front entrance.

Hair tousled and wearing work clothes covered in mold and stained with bleach, Dona runs to the desk in the high school's reception foyer.

Jane-Claire's upperclassman acquaintances who are office aides give her a full eyewitness account about her mom later.

"Dona Stevens, Lerue Stevens's mom. Have you found him?" Her words tumble out in staccato between heaving breaths of air.

"No, ma'am. The attendance office called up after third period," the older lady speaks in the slow drawl of North Alabama. Dona waves her hand in the air in an effort to speed the lady along.

"What about the library? Lerue and J.C. tutor the

refugee group." She's not about to accept "No" for an answer.

"You could check." How many syllables can the receptionist squeeze into three words?

Dona snatches a Visitor sticker and flies down the hall. She peeks in classes already in session as if a mother's homing instinct is capable of finding her children anywhere.

The library's double doors loom in front of her, and she stops just as she clears the entrance. She holds onto the frame and scans the students inside.

Lerue sits at a table with D'wayne going over math problems. He sees his mom and immediately moves to intercept. "Mom, what are you doing here?"

Dona seizes Lerue's arm just to make sure he's real. "Kit called... Because the attendance office. . .. She was so sure you left for Gulfport."

"And you believed her?" Lerue frowns. "Why do you always assume the worst about everything?"

Dona laughs. "Do you really have to ask that?"

"Yeah, I hear you." Lerue shrugs.

D'wayne stands and walks over next to Lerue. He's so big that even Lerue appears stunted.

Lerue steps back to include him, all of him, in the circle.

"Mom, this is D'wayne Duplancais. He's from New Orleans." D'wayne smiles as he wraps Dona in a big bear hug. "We family, Ms. Stevens. J.C. say you from the Big Easy. What high school you go to?"

Dona tries her best to breathe normally and smiles in spite of herself. It's been a long while since she's heard a true Ninth Ward Yat accent.

"St. James Major on Gentilly Boulevard by Franklin. It

was just a small girls school. We only had thirty-two in our graduating class."

Suddenly, Dona stops. Her smile fades and her eyes narrow, switching back and forth between Lerue and D'wayne. "Wait a minute, where's J.C.?"

D'wayne's eyes pop. Jane-Claire couldn't be more busted if she tried.

Lerue rolls his eyes and crosses his arms in front of him.

"She's on her way to Gulfport." He tells his mom the absolute truth. Jane-Claire never set foot in school today. She dropped him off and left hours ago, but Dona insists on dragging him downstairs and scouring the student parking lot.

Dona walks row after row in the southern asphalt heat while Lerue waits in the alumni plaza.

Only after she walks the entire student parking lot does she join him. She takes his arm and tries to pull him back inside the school, but Lerue plays like dead meat. She can't make him budge one step.

He has her attention. Then he offers her the deal.

IN AN EXAM ROOM AT MEMORIAL, Mason frowns. Gulfport's changed since the storm. He says it over and over. He compares it to a wild west town where opportunity and lawlessness reign.

Volunteers flood the area but also a subclass of people who are only looking to make a buck from pain and the misery of disaster. One guy slaps a roofer sign on his truck. Another buys a chainsaw and charges a fortune to clear downed trees. Mold experts crawl from under any rock. All predators gravitating to weakened distracted prey.

Mason works under a bright spotlight to suture a

wound in a middle-aged roughneck's hand. He's alone in the room with the man.

Just as Mason is about to finish, the roughneck speaks for the first time since the procedure began.

"So, do you feel it?" His breath reeks of booze. The time is barely past noon.

"Feel what? I got all the glass out." Mason can't pick and choose which exam room he enters or what patient he examines. Moving from one to the other, he takes what he gets.

"No, out there. Do you feel civilization peeling away?" The weathered roughneck laughs. His spit lands in the sterile field.

Mason laughs instead of looking at the man. He wants to finish and get to the next patient. He doesn't want to hear this man's philosophy.

The weathered roughneck doesn't laugh. He stares straight ahead into nothing.

"You know what I feel? Another long ass shift." Mason dodges the confrontation and wipes his brow on his scrub shirt.

"The devil's taking over out there. His territory now." The roughneck grunts.

Nurse Lori peers in the exam room. "Dr. Stevens, another one. I put her in GYN."

"I'll be there as soon as I can, get the kit ready." Mason hates that rape seems to be one of the most prolific byproducts of the disaster. He thinks of Jane-Claire. Dona.

The roughneck chuckles.

Mason glances at the man. "What are you laughing at?"

"Feel it now?" The roughneck grins at Mason.

Mason refocuses and just finishes his sewing job when

his cellphone rings. He doesn't get many calls and forgot to turn it on silent. He exits the exam room to answer.

"Dona?" Mason is relieved to escape the room, but Dona never calls him during a shift. Not even if she's in labor. He stands in the hallway and presses near the wall.

"Jane-Claire's driving Lerue's car. She's headed to Gulfport." Dona's voice shakes with tension.

"Why'd you let her do that?" Mason hisses into the cellphone.

"I didn't let her do anything. I didn't know anything about it." Her anxious voice fires into the cellphone.

"Can't you catch up with her? Stop her somehow?" Mason wonders why she called him with this. What is he supposed to do?

"She's got over two hours head start, Mason. Get someone to take the rest of your shift and go meet her. She's probably going to the house."

Mason listens then looks up and down the hall. "How the hell am I supposed to do that?"

Back at the high school, Dona stands on the curb between the alumni plaza and the student parking lot. She paces between two brick columns.

"I don't care how you do it. It'll be dark by the time she gets there."

"I don't know." Mason sounds noncommittal, whiny.

"Well, I do." Dona fumes. "You didn't bother to get off for my mother's funeral. Are you totally absolved from helping your family because of patients? Are you a doctor or a father?"

"Dona, you're upset."

"Damn right I am."

"Why aren't you and Lerue on your way down? Why aren't you going after her?"

"Because I have a damn wreck of a car that's about to

croak and Lerue made me an offer I can't refuse. We'll leave as soon as his college applications are done." Dona glances at Lerue who leans casually against a brick column. "Right, Lerue?"

"Yes ma'am, that's the deal. J.C. said she needed some time." Lerue stands glued to the same spot in the shade near the column.

Dona holds the phone close. "Mason, there will always be more patients. But we're the only family you have. If you want to keep us, you have a choice to make." She closes the call.

Mason stands in the hallway and looks at the phone in his hand.

Lori exit an exam room. He grabs her arm. "Lori, I need you to call Dr. Wells. Tell him I have a family emergency. I need his help."

Mason doesn't wait for an answer.

SIXTEEN

Coastal Destruction

Jane-Claire left Gulfport with her family because everything was destroyed. She's on her way back to salvage her most important treasure.

She has to go see Natalie even if Nat hasn't written her one letter and doesn't even want to see her anymore.

What would she be if she doesn't?

The thread between them is frayed but if she lets the connection go, she will truly have nothing left. None of them would.

The drive is white knuckle time the whole way and seems longer because she has no one to follow. Mom will be angry. Jane-Claire hopes she'll understand.

The miles seem to recede like a mirage in front of her. She pats the violin case beside her in the passenger seat. At least, she's not alone.

She is cautious, but stays with the traffic through Birmingham because she doesn't want to call attention to herself. She listens to country music and black Bible thumping preachers. She prays, but she's not sure that her faith is strong enough to believe that all will be well.

In the road glare, her eyes sting, burn. She didn't sleep the night before. In her dreams, the violin was screaming as high and wild as the wind of the hurricane.

She stops at all the rest areas. She fumbles at the pump but manages to refill the gas tank of the car. She pays in cash. Her lids get heavy. Lulled. Jane-Claire must stay awake, alert. She needs to get there.

As she enters Mississippi, Jane-Claire gulps two paper bathroom cups of hospitality coffee at the welcome station even though she's not a coffee drinker. The bitter liquid sweetened with too much sugar and powder cream revs her for the last stretch.

By the time she approaches the coast, the sun rides low on the horizon and autumn shadows range across the road. The sky is a brilliant orange. Jane-Claire muses that she might be an over the road driver after all.

Then she enters the dead zone. Even from Highway 49 in the Passport moving at the speed limit, the blight cannot be missed the closer she gets to the coast. She drives past an enormous junkyard of derelict cars, and another of destroyed pleasure boats.

Almost every house has blue tarp covering damage to the roof, and trees toppled in the yard. Piles of shattered lumber are everywhere. Fences are down. She is in the apocalypse.

The sunset afterglow is almost gone by the time she parallel parks Lerue's Honda against the railroad tracks. Jane-Claire's Second Street neighborhood is dark and abandoned. Exhausted, she exits the car.

Although the raised railbed leading to Second Street acts as a lure, her mission takes priority. She turns inland, to the interior and the old neighborhood where Memaw lives. Jane-Claire heads to Memaw's house and has no idea that her dad stews in parental torment as he waits for her in the ruins of their house.

MASON SITS on a wooden crate in front of a cardboard dish pack box that acts as a makeshift desk. He shuffles through a load of bills but doesn't touch the checkbook lying in the far corner.

Bituminous rubs against his leg. He reaches down, absently scratches the black cat's neck and under his chin. Bit purrs like a motorboat. Mason picks the cat up, cradles him like an infant, and hugs him. The stack of bills falls – splat - to the floor.

The living room where Mason sits is mostly clear of furniture and debris. The sheetrock has been removed up to the water line, about four feet up, to expose the wooden studs underneath. The wall separating the living room and the master bedroom is gone. Garbage still litters the rest of the house.

Camouflaged among the broken pieces of sheet rock and broken wood in the master bedroom is a six-foot-long Burmese python, one of the finest in Miss Adele's collection.

The snake slithers along the floorboard, then between mounds of rubbish. Although the snake moves with silent stealth, a suspicious shuffling sound from disturbed trash catches Mason's attention.

Mason bolts upright and dumps the cat on the floor. He listens to the muffled jogging of the debris and pulls the handgun from his pocket. He bought the model that the policemen who often visit the emergency department recommended along with their preferred hollow-point bullets. The cops gave their best advice with maximum damage in mind. These bullets are designed to stop someone. They are made to kill. The exit wound is much bigger because the bullets explode on impact.

Mason never considered himself capable of hurting anyone or anything. He grew up in Alabama, but was never a hunting enthusiast yet, here he is, checking a gun he just purchased to make sure it is loaded.

The trauma of losing everything, these dangerous days changed him. He would hurt something to protect himself and his family.

Mason trudges through the absent boundary between the living room and the master bedroom. He kicks errant pieces of garbage back into the bedroom, as if the material is trying to purposefully ooze into the cleared living room.

A piece of sheetrock hits the snake.

Bit meows, runs in front of Mason, and trips him up.

"Damn cat." He knee jerks Bit out of his way and into the path of the snake. Bituminous snarls and curves his back like a Halloween cat, skips sideways and circles the room.

Mason pulls his cellphone from his pocket, sniffs the dead atmosphere, then murmurs, "It's got to be in here." He reverses direction, stuffing the cellphone into one pants pocket and the gun in the other and retreats to the living room.

He grabs a flashlight and returns to the bedroom. He shines the beam into the debris and uses the steel toe of his boot to sift through layers of garbage and broken furniture.

Rancid dust stirs into a pint size cloud. Pushing aside a red surfboard that looks as if it were bitten in two by a giant shark, he unearths an unblemished china plate from Dona's wedding pattern.

Mason picks it up and places it to the side on the floor, out of harm's way, then returns to the hunt.

The snake creeps into the darkness under the smelly

king size mattress and coils around a pale cylindrical object hidden beneath the soggy memory foam.

Mason zeros in and tries one-handed to upend the mattress, but the wet material is way too heavy. Suddenly, voices drift from beyond the tarp covered window at the front of the house.

He turns, touches the gun tucked in his pocket, and postpones his search to march into the living room. He calls loudly and what he hopes comes off as aggressive, "You insurance adjusters have some nerve. Ever heard of trespassing?"

A middle-aged couple dressed in resort clothes wave at Mason, and continue through the blown out front window they just used as an entrance into the house. "Hello there, I'm Jack Mays. This is my better half, Terry."

Dona flashes through Mason's mind. His best half. He staggers under the reproach and failure of his visit the day before. "What the hell do you want? This is my home you just walked into. . . Uninvited."

"We're from Virginia Beach." Terry, Jack's wife, ignores Mason's comment and offers their hometown as explanation. "Your house is the only one on the whole block still standing."

Mason peers at the woman. His mouth is a thin line and his tone confrontational. "Tell me something I don't know."

The woman opens her arms and gestures. "It looks like your house is built on two lots."

Mason is baffled, unable to follow her logic. "So what?"

Jack touches the studs on the wall. "Still wet. I bet estimates on black mold remediation are out of sight."

Mason sighs in spite of himself. The week before he met with an expert on black mold who explained the entire lengthy process of remediation to him. He was still in sticker shock.

Jack surveys the living room. "All the wood has to be dried completely or the treatment's useless."

"I know." Mason stands immobile, unable to comprehend why these people are here and what they want from him.

"Interested in selling?" The words roll off the man's tongue and hit Mason squarely.

He walks to the tarp covering the open bay window at the front of the house. "I'm planning to rebuild." Mason makes his statement with as much conviction as he can muster.

The Mays laugh and humiliate Mason in his own home. His hand slips to the gun in his pocket. For a flash moment, he knows what it feels like to want to kill someone.

Terry meanders to the missing interior wall between the living room and the master bedroom. "This is still quite a shamble."

"You should have seen it." Mason removes his hand from his pocket, and pulls back the tarp to open the exit. The evening breeze from the beach blows through the opening into the living room.

He gazes out to the Gulf, still amazed that he can see the shoreline which was not possible before the storm. The view is the one perk that he counts as a positive, even if the price was too high.

"Would you be agreeable to an offer?" Jack strolls closer. Terry circles Mason in the opposite direction. Predators moving in triangulation.

"I don't know. I'm supposed to meet with a friend's brother, a contractor, this evening."

Terry and Jack exchange a knowing look.

"Fat chance with that." The woman mocks as she throws her comment at Mason.

Jack steps up. "Land's expected to skyrocket but you'll have to wait awhile. We believe the neighborhood will rebuild but with prefab homes. Something more temporary." He pulls his business card and hands it to Mason. "Think about it. Weigh your options. Give me a call if you want to talk." Jack offers his hand.

Mason doesn't take it. The couple exit through the blown-out window. He walks back inside to collapse in a green plastic chair, hanging his head in his hands. This is too much to think of all at once. Where is she?

IN THE DEEP DUSK, Jane-Claire walks the street to Memaw's house. She carries the violin case and her camera in the gadget bag. Trees lost limbs but still stand. Cars park bumper to bumper along the curb.

Jane-Claire has only been to Memaw's house one time before, and she doesn't think she'll be any more welcome this time than last. She stops in front of a neat frame house set on a narrow lot.

Standing at the front gate, she pats the violin case strapped to her back. The instrument has been with her for weeks now. After that night when she upended Natalie in the linen closet, she thought that if she kept the violin, that her friendship with Natalie would survive intact and unchanged.

But the violin haunts her.

Originally a symbol of trust, it only serves now as a reminder that nothing was the same and everything had changed. Why should her friendship with Natalie be any different?

Jane-Claire takes the violin case and her gadget bag

from her back and holds them by the handles at her sides. Natalie was a good friend and she would always honor that as a true fact of her past, if not her future. She is as prepared as she can be.

She glances down at the violin case.

"Hey. . . Say goodbye. Time to go home."

A fence surrounds the perimeter of Memaw's house, and Jane-Claire hopes that the old woman doesn't keep a mean dog in the yard. She waits and looks before opening the gate and going up the steps of the stoop.

A porch swing gently sways in the breeze off the Gulf. She smells the salt water and the sickening, sweet odor of decay.

Her knock on the door stirs whispers and footsteps within the house. The yellow porch light flips on, and she backs up so whoever is looking through the peephole inside can see her clearly.

But nothing happens. Jane-Claire recalls her visit to Miss Adele before the hurricane. The old lady was on the other side and she wasn't going to open it.

She tries again. "Natalie? Memaw? It's me. It's Jane-Claire." She steps back again into the circle created by the glow of the yellow bug light.

The door cracks open. Natalie peeks through the slit, unsure if Jane-Claire is nothing but a hallucination or apparition.

"Is it really you?" Nat's voice is timid, hoarse as if she hasn't spoken in a long time.

"Who else?" Jane-Claire's temper sparks and she blurts out. "Nat, is everything okay?" Probably the stupidest question ever asked that she repeats way too often. Try again. "Open up. Aren't you going to let me in?"

Jane-Claire waits an absurdly long time before Natalie

opens the door. She's lost weight like everyone who was in the storm.

Memaw has her hair screwed up into poppyotts. Nat looks pale and wears a wrist brace.

"How are you? How long do you have to wear that?" Jane-Claire gestures to the brace and blinks to fight rising tears.

"Jane-Claire?" Natalie's eyes are open but she's not seeing what's in front of her. "Why are you here?"

That, Jane-Claire has an answer to… "Because of you." She hugs Natalie who stands like a post. "Look what I brought. Your violin misses you." She shoves the violin into Nat's arms.

Natalie takes the case and immediately puts it on the floor beside the entrance. She opens the door.

Jane-Claire drops her gadget bag next to the violin and follows her into the house. The girls sit together in the living room.

Memaw appears and clucks a little but seems agreeable to seeing Jane-Claire. She brings the girls milk and peanut butter balls that are homemade and wonderful.

J.C. eats them like she's starving, thankful that Memaw still views them as children even if she's wrong.

"So, what's going on?" Jane-Claire asks Nat the simple question and her friend who always has a million words to share, sits, says nothing, and only touches one of the wonderful goodies after Jane-Claire coaxes her by pressing the soft confection into her hand.

"I don't talk about it." She won't look Jane-Claire in the face, much less the eye.

"Have you heard from your Momma?" Jane-Claire pushes, because if she doesn't, who will?

Natalie shakes her head and whispers, "Memaw and

196

Mom don't get along. The day of the storm, a tornado hit our house."

"I saw it, Nat. I was one address away." Jane-Claire shudders at the flood of memories.

"One minute I was with Bit, then the next, I was in the debris. That's how I hurt my arm." Natalie raises her arm. "The brace comes off next week, but then I don't have any excuse." Natalie hyperventilates as if the thought of recovery is loathsome.

Jane-Claire doesn't understand. She sits and listens.

"Momma brought me to the hospital, then Memaw came. She says mom left for the Veteran's Hospital." Nat speaks as if she doesn't want Memaw to hear, but the old woman stands at the doorframe.

Memaw blends with the dark in the hallway beyond. Her wizened hands clasp her face, and she shakes her head back and forth in slow walk tempo. Tears glisten on the old woman's dark oily skin.

"Did your mom get there?" Jane-Claire tries to imagine how that would have even been possible. Miss Shirin would have had to walk back from the hospital, navigate half a block of storm surge, climb an eight-foot fence, and go another half block to get to the Veteran's Hospital.

"Memaw says she did. She says Momma was washed out of a second story window then was airlifted to a hospital in Hattiesburg. Memaw says she's still there because of depression and shock." Natalie finally looks at Jane-Claire. Her face is fierce, angry. "I don't believe her." She spits the words at her friend.

Jane-Claire tries to downplay her rage, but fury is real, potent, and tempting. Anger delivers a burning energy and purpose, especially when nothing is there to take its place. Rage possesses. "Why would Memaw lie to you?"

Then as quickly as Natalie's anger manifests, all emotion drains from her face. She looks brain dead. "Memaw says cell coverage is sketch. Mail is worse, but I did get your letters. We stood in line for hours. Memaw says school won't start until after Thanksgiving." She speaks in a monotone like a robot.

Jane-Claire wants to shake Natalie, maybe even slap her, but she sits on her hands. "What do you say?"

Natalie looks down. Tears spring from her eyes. "I pray that Mom went to find my Dad, but I think that might just be a dream inside a nightmare."

Jane-Claire questions that as a valid possibility. "Been a long time since you saw your Dad. Since you were little." From what Jane-Claire heard about the man, he was foreign, German, and super handsome. Shirin worshiped him, and he left her pregnant and ridiculed by her own family. She never saw the man again.

Outside the front window, Jane-Claire sees that it's full dark now. Fear creeps close.

"I have to go. My dad might be waiting for me at the house. Mom must've called him by now. I can come back in the morning, but only if you want me too." Jane-Claire takes Nat's hand. She is cold, unresponsive. "Nat, you've been in the dead zone. The world really does start to look normal again. A friend told me it will, it just takes time."

Natalie looks at Jane-Claire. Yes, straight in the eye. Her anger boils just below the surface. "A friend? You've already made friends?" She acts betrayed. She's ready to believe the worst, as if the worst is all there is to believe.

"My teacher. School does give you something to do. That helps." Jane-Claire looks at Natalie, regretful that she was so ready to accuse her of the same disloyalty. "Want to come with me to my house?"

She has no idea these words will trigger pure panic.

Natalie screams. She recoils and contracts into a ball. Her eyes over open in alarm. "No, I can't. I haven't been back. I can't go over there."

Jane-Claire hasn't been back over there either, but she refrains from pointing that out.

"Stay here if..." Natalie's voice trails off, and Jane-Claire can tell that she is thinking of her own dad.

"If he's not there. Thanks." Jane-Claire appreciates her offer. She gets up to leave.

Natalie catches her arm. "Wait. I have something." She leaves the room, quickly returns and hands Jane-Claire two things. . . the journal and all her letters.

Jane-Claire is flabbergasted. She looks down at the worn book where all the memories of her past life reside. Despite everything she's been going through, her journal has never been too far from her thoughts.

"You had it?" Then Jane-Claire's relieved happiness crashes. All of her letters to Natalie are unopened. "You didn't read my letters? Why? Nat, what the heck's going on with you?"

Natalie puddles. "I don't deserve your letters. It's a lot of work being first chair violin. You end up being responsible for everyone's mistakes. If I'm first chair, then someone else is second. Is that fair? My conductor keeps calling Memaw to find out if I'm practicing and something about rehearsing before school starts. I can't do that."

She talks gibberish as far as Jane-Claire is concerned. She grabs her shoulders. "If you say can't then you can't! You have to try."

Natalie shakes her head. "I'm scared. I might not be able to. When you came to me in the hospital, I was so mean. I was angry about my arm. I'm sorry. Keep it for me. A little longer."

"No, I brought it home today. It's yours." Jane-Claire

hugs Natalie. She's been around Lerue and her mom enough to know how bad, worthless, and little disaster can make you feel. "Do not apologize for anything. We're all good." And she truly means it.

"I don't remember much about that night... Except I put Bituminous in the cat carrier." A gut sob escapes Natalie. Tears flow, and her eyes look red and burned. "He drowned. I drowned my cat."

Jane-Claire smiles and shakes her head. "No. I told you that night at the hospital. I saw Bit. My dad's seen him since. He brings food to him. Bit's fine."

"He's alive?" Natalie blinks, then shuts down. People write their own history of the disaster and will not change it, even in the face of fact. "He can't be... No. Bit died, and it was my fault. I put him in the carrier."

"Believe me." Jane-Claire laughs. "I saw him. He's okay. Nat?"

Natalie crashes to the couch, hangs her head, and doubles over. She wraps her arms around her knees and rocks back and forth. "No, Bit's dead. I put him in the carrier, and he drowned. He's dead and gone with everything else."

Jane-Claire reaches down and lays her journal and the unopened letters beside Natalie. She talks in a gentle, calm voice, "Keep my journal. Just a little while longer. And can you keep my video camera tonight? Protect them. And read the letters because I wrote them for you."

Jane-Claire kisses Natalie's hair and turns to leave. Memaw even waves. The opaque landscape of Second Street rises against the midnight blue sky above the Gulf. She hopes her dad waits for her.

SEVENTEEN

Mold and Memory Foam

At the top of the raised railbed, Jane-Claire has a clear unobstructed view of the Gulf. Her eyes gradually adjust to the dark.

Scant moonlight dances on shallow wavelets far out into the water and glosses over her scrubbed raw neighborhood. Giant mounds of debris wait to be hauled away.

Her house is the only structure in sight.

Candlelight shines yellow and flickering from the back windows. Her dad must be there, and her emotions tumble.

She yearns for her "before" dad. She wants to hug him and talk to him in that pre-storm moment just before he left for the hurricane shift, as if all this never happened.

But she's come this far and nothing with Natalie was what she imagined it would be. If there's still a chance with Nat, then there's still hope for her dad.

Jane-Claire scrambles down the embankment. Lost in thought, she doesn't spot the double rows of razor wire, the circular kind used on prison fences, until she is right on top of the treacherous obstacle.

She freezes in place and scans up and down the barrier. The wire runs the length of the railbed and, from what she can see, encircles the entire neighborhood. There's no way for her to cross without getting cut to ribbons, and she has no idea if, or where, checkpoints can be found. There might even be a curfew. She breaks out in a sweat. To be so close. She wrestles with the rush of frustration and anger then the sound of muffled voices.

Startled, she crawls over a felled oak limb near the obstacle and hides in a heap of leaves. She digs in, determined to stay still even as the soaking layers of held humidity make her itch. She says a silent prayer that there is no poison ivy growing in the hollow.

Three men chuckle as they approach the razor wire. One holds tin snips. Another carries a bolt cutter, and the third cradles a fifth of Jack Daniels in his arms. They point to the candle in her house and laugh.

Jane-Claire worries that her house is their target. The looters make easy work of the protective barrier, cutting the wire like butter and putting on gloves to pull it back to access. She would have never guessed the barrier was so easy to penetrate. Symbolic, not functional.

A low hum plays in the night. Nearby insects. The bark on the tree limb strangely shimmers and she struggles not to scream as she perceives the wood roaches crawling by the hundreds over the limb.

She questions which is worse - looters or roaches - to help focus and control her rapid breathing. As the men move away from her and down the street, her terror subsides.

Jane-Claire waits until they are out of ear shot, then tightropes over the felled oak limb. She moves quickly, crushing some of the roaches under her shoes, to the place where the looters cut the razor wire.

She steps through the opening into her own backyard and feels like she's sneaking into a cemetery. The candlelight beckons her, but thankful for the moonlight, she plots a path to avoid nails or glass hidden in the sandy dirt.

When she steps onto the catawampus back porch, the decking, warped by its encounter with salty sea water, yields a mournful creak.

The kitchen door is barred shut so she enters the house through the back door that leads into her parents' room. Filled with rubbish, the master bedroom is pretty gnarly.

Jane-Claire is traversing the debris field again as she balances on wobbly fragments of unrecognizable stuff.

She freezes. Her dad is talking with someone in the living room. Jane-Claire hops from the broken top of the antique sewing machine onto the soggy king size mattress.

"I was expecting to meet your brother." Her dad's voice is cautious.

"He left yesterday. His wife said he better get his tail home, or there wasn't going to be any home to come back to." Jane-Claire recognizes the woman's voice. One of the nurses. She remembered dad told mom that one of the nurses had a brother who was a contractor.

"I was hoping he would at least give me an estimate. Some idea of where to start." He sounds genuinely bothered. "This is the third appointment I've had this week. No one shows."

Jane-Claire grimaces and looks down. She has sunk up to her ankles into the wet memory foam.

A terrible stench rises from the ruined mattress. Covering her mouth with her hand, she suffocates rather than breathe in the smell.

"Three for three then. Why put money into this place? I have a trailer all set up." The woman's silky voice implies more than her words say.

"I guess it's just something else to get used to. The new normal."

Good for you, Dad. Jane-Claire mentally comments on the conversation as she listens. Act dumb. Get her out of here. Quick. She sways, faint and dizzy.

"My kids love Hattiesburg. Grandma cooks and cleans and helps with homework, plus their daddy doesn't argue with her."

"So what!" Jane-Claire nearly yells at the woman when she recognizes the voice as Lori Sandt. No wonder her son pierces himself and dyes his hair orange. She doesn't even see him. She doesn't miss him. Jane-Claire aches all over. She holds her stomach. Is she sick? Or is she just sick of all this?

She scans the room. Ragged water marks the sheetrock. Mom's writing desk in pieces. A cock-eyed abstract painting on the wall, one that mom's mother painted for her, with an old tall ship sailing off into an unknown infinite landscape.

She silently pleads for Mrs. Sandt to leave so she can quit balancing on the nasty mattress.

But she listens and waits for her dad. He needs to tell that woman to go. He has to be the one to do it. Otherwise, Jane-Claire will never know the truth. She makes a bet with herself. Dad says no to this woman. If he doesn't, she takes her chances and goes back to Memaw's house to spend the night with Natalie, and she tells mom. If he somehow says yes, he explodes a marriage Jane-Claire looks on as rocky but near perfect.

If that happens, everything truly will be lost.

"Kids are pretty pragmatic. They go with the flow." Mason's voice is low, measured.

Jane-Claire wonders whether he is being evasive or if

that is what he really believes, that his family is nothing but little freeloaders looking for the best deal?

"Maybe we should take a lesson from them." Jane-Claire can hear the woman's smile. "Maybe they're better off in their new homes. Maybe we're better off without them."

Jane-Claire can't hold still. She looks down at the holes made by her sinking shoes.

Maybe that woman is a terrible mom and a bitch to boot. She doesn't even know them. What is she talking about?

Mason's shoes scrape the wooden floor as he backs away. "I don't believe I'm that easily forgotten by my family."

No, he's not. Jane-Claire swats tears running down her face and pictures Lerue crying on Saturday afternoons.

"I'm already divorced." Isn't that convenient? She's all ready to go.

"Well, last I looked I'm not." Jane-Claire tries to breathe. Between getting sick, crying, and the stench, she's totally stopped up.

Mason walks to the window and shows Mrs. Sandt the door. The plastic tarp crinkles as he pulls it back and the woman's athletic shoes squeak on her way out.

BUT BEFORE JANE-CLAIRE can mush her way out of the decomposing king size gunk, he's on the phone and talking to mom. "Where the hell is she? I can't stay any longer. It's getting late. They stole the copper backsplash in back of the stove last night. Okay. Okay."

Jane-Claire's shoes are stuck in the memory foam. The stuff is like quicksand. She sinks deeper, in over her ankles, toward the floor.

Suddenly, something moves under her feet beneath the bottom fabric of the mattress.

She panics and plunges her hands into the slimy quagmire to release the velcro straps of her Teva sandals.

Jane-Claire jumps from her shoes, trapped by the playdoh mess and lands on the floor. She takes her first step and jabs a random splinter into her foot. A single yelp escapes.

She doesn't realize that she just set off a firestorm.

"Shit. I'll call back." Mason hears the noise from the master bedroom and flips the cellphone closed. He jerks the gun out of his pocket and release the gun safety in one move.

"What? Ya didn't get it all? There's nothing left." Mason bellows his challenge and charges through the gap between the living room and master bedroom.

The splinter hurts. Jane-Claire bends over and tries to pull it out but her hands are slippery with mattress goo. Her dad rages in the other room.

Her mouth opens, but nothing comes out. Possibly a stupid squeak, but nothing near enough intelligible to identify herself in the cluttered dark.

"Get the hell out of my house." Mason yells as loud as he can.

Mason clears the hole punched in the wall between the rooms. His face is wild and super focused at the same time. Visions of the looters at the fence and the creeper Randy flash through her mind. Their laughter echoes in the silence.

Dad is only defending his home. Dad is nuts.

Mason raises the gun and takes a deadeye aim.

Jane-Claire can't believe this is happening. He points the gun straight at her. Her eyes saucer. She lifts her filthy arms, crossing them in front of her.

"Dad, no. It's me." Her voice doesn't sound right, but she pushes the words out. The air fighting to break through her vocal cords. "Dad, no."

Mason gasps. He drops the gun as if it suddenly transformed into a red-hot poker.

The gun hits the floor and fires. Bullets explode into the soggy memory foam. A million pieces fly like dirty snow throughout the room.

Jane-Claire crouches down, covers her head with her arms, and screams in cadence. She can't stop screaming.

"Jane-Claire. Baby." Mason crashes to the floor and he crawls on his knees through the detritus to his daughter. "God help me, Jane-Claire. I'm sorry. I am so sorry," Mason chokes a sob and takes her in his arms. He sees the blood on her hands and searches for the source. "Are you okay? Are you hurt? Oh, Jesus."

Jane-Claire stops screaming and raises her dirty, bloody foot to show him the splinter.

Mason removes the sharp wooden shard in one practiced move. He tears a piece from his green scrub shirt, wraps the fabric around Jane-Claire's wound then hugs her again.

"Will you get me a cellphone now? I could have called you." Jane-Claire admits to herself that this is unscrupulous on her part, but she just can't bear seeing her dad's face so full of emotion. She has never before seen him cry.

"Yeah, baby. Sure thing." They cling to each other and for two seconds, the ordeal is over. Everything will be alright.

Then a raspy, scraping sound from under what's left of the mattress.

Bituminous hisses and arches his back but keeps his distance from the gooey mound.

Mason zips to high alert. He examines the room, sniffs. "Stay by me, J.C. Something's here."

Jane-Claire is about to tell him about the movement she felt underneath the mattress, when they hear the sound again.

Mason helps her stand. They back from the room as far as the absent wall. Mason nudges the gun with the tip of his shoe, pushing it to the side as if the gun is alive. He makes sure the barrel points away from them.

"What is it?" Jane-Claire combs the moonlit darkness. The grating scratchy noise grows louder.

"Death. I smell it." Mason glares at the mattress, same as Jane-Claire.

Bituminous snarls and crouches low to the floor. He advances in spurts like a hunter on his prey.

Mason steps in front of Jane-Claire and picks up a flashlight.

She holds onto her dad's arm. "I smelled that as soon as I drove across the interstate. That sticky sweet smell. It's all over down here." Talking makes her feel better. Maybe a little.

"Not this smell. This is close. Stay back." Mason shines the light beam across the rubble of the bedroom. "Here, hold it for me." He hands Jane-Claire the flashlight and points to the mattress. "The sound's coming from underneath."

Mason grabs the mattress with both hands and flips it over to expose... the Burmese Python.

"Shit!" Mason vaults back and bounces into Jane-Claire. They both end up on their butts on the floor. Jane-Claire screams really loud this time. She throws the flashlight at the snake. Not the best move since now they can't see too well.

Bituminous's snarl is primeval. The cat attacks the

snake and sinks his teeth into the coils at the back of the snake's head.

The python seems impervious to Bit and slithers forward, dragging not only the cat but a prize discovered under the mattress.

"Back up. Back up." Mason waves his arms. He bounces to his feet and dances around the fighting animals.

Jane-Claire clambers up and limps to retrieve a packing box.

Mason seizes the snake by the tail and wrestles the weighted coil of muscle away from the pale cylinder. Straining, he pulls the snake, cat, and debris toward the box.

The dirt and dust of the room stirs into a foggy miasma. Mason and Jane-Claire gasp and choke on the polluted air. They can barely see.

Suddenly, Mason stops and stiffens. He drops the snake and sniffs the cloudy putrid air.

Jane-Claire snatches the flashlight and shines it on the snake's prize. Her hands feel like putty as she comprehends what the snake has wrapped in its coils. "No, no!"

"Dear God, get away. Get back." Mason grabs the flashlight from her and beats the snake. He stomps the heel of his tennis shoe into the coils until the snake releases the human remains in its grasp.

Jane-Claire tilts the empty box to its side and grabs a broom used for cleanup. She bats Bituminous from the snake and helps her dad scoop and sweep the snake into the box.

Mason pushes the box upright and tapes the box shut. They stand winded, dirty, and in shock then turn to the decomposed body of a woman with a nest of wild tangled hair.

Mason tries to turn Jane-Claire's face away. He holds her tight and they sink to the floor.

"I knew it. I told the coroner I smelled human remains. He came out once, but they stopped looking when he found a dead seal in the backyard. Jane-Claire? You okay? J.C.? Why? Poor soul." Mason buries his head in Jane-Claire's shoulder. Wracked pent up sobs escape.

But Jane-Claire can't look away. She can't take her eyes off the woman's hair. "It's Natalie's mom.... It's Miss Shirin."

Jane-Claire sits at the gaping hole in the wall and keeps vigil over the body, now covered by one of her mom's best tablecloths, while she and her dad wait late into the night for the coroner to come and take the body away.

She is cried out long before she pushes her sore feet back into her grimy river sandals and they are finally able to leave. They take Mason's truck back to Memorial.

Armed National Guard troops encamp in a ring around the entire perimeter of the hospital. Jane-Claire clings to her dad's arm as they pass a check point to enter. No one asks for her learner's permit this time.

Mason still inhabits the echocardiography room. That night, Jane-Claire sleeps on the same gurney used to park the dead after the storm, but her dad sits beside her and holds her hand, so all is okay.

EIGHTEEN

Inching Back

The next morning, Jane-Claire and Mason sit across from each other in the infamous hospital cafeteria. Her mom would say that was adversarial, but Jane-Claire doesn't agree. She would say that they had come to a truce.

She loves her dad, even if she doesn't always agree with him. Like now. They pretend to eat breakfast but really, they push food around their plates.

"So, I can't say anything to Natalie?" Jane-Claire went to sleep pondering the gruesome events of the night. She dreamed about the body in her parents' bedroom and woke with Miss Shirin on her mind.

"Nothing." Mason doesn't hesitate, and in fact, he states his answer as a direct command. "Not a word until the coroner is able to make a positive identification."

Jane-Claire doesn't respond. His gag order bothers her big time and she wears her best mean face. That makes her dad uncomfortable, so she pushes a little. "You saw her hair. It's Miss Shirin."

Mason can't take Jane-Claire's recrimination. He had his own dreams last night. Dreams of massive blood loss and a beloved child dead by his own hand. "It's been weeks, J.C. We just don't know for sure."

Jane-Claire considers herself warned and changes the subject. Sort of. "How do you think she died? The storm was done and Memaw says someone at the VA saw her."

Jane-Claire imagines breaking the news to Natalie. She has no idea how she would, but she doesn't know how to keep the news from her either. The grief, disbelief, and horror will be just another disaster steamrolling over her.

"Bad people take advantage of chaos in a disaster. We'll find the answer. But you have to promise me you won't say anything to Natalie. Please. You can't do that. We don't know. Promise me." Mason smiles and takes hold of Jane-Claire's chin. "You're a good actress, as well as a film maker. Keep this to yourself until we have the proof. Win the Oscar."

Jane-Claire looks down at the hospital food. The scrambled eggs look like spilled brains. She fights a wave of nausea and remembers listening while the police put the body into the black plastic bag. She couldn't bring herself to look but she heard the grown men grunting and trying not to spill expletives about decay and dismemberment.

She prays for Miss Shirin and wishes she had a hundred red Community Coffee cans full of weed to give her. Jane-Claire concentrates her thoughts on today and how she can keep a straight face with Natalie.

"I need Bituminous. I need a prop to help keep me focused." The cat is a spontaneous thought, but it might work as a distraction.

Mason looks down. "Jane-Claire. Last night." He doesn't need to say anymore.

Her dad doesn't want her to tell mom what happened. While they waited for the coroner, dad recovered the gun, unloaded it, and took it apart as much as he could.

"Do you think I can forget it?" Jane-Claire looks up at Mason and suddenly agrees with her mom. Sitting across from someone is combative. "You almost shot me with that stupid gun."

"No." Mason answers quick and sure. "For God's sake, I could have killed you." The guilt of what might have happened presses on him. The weight is visible from across the table.

"I won't tell if you won't rag mom about not evacuating to the hospital. She's really sorry and you won't let it go. You bring it up every time you talk to her. I don't want to hear you say anything about it ever again."

Jane-Claire leans over the table, surprised by her ferocity. And don't forget the cellphone, she wants to add that, but she trusts him to remember.

"You almost killed me." Jane-Claire stops and collects her temper. "But you didn't. Just like we didn't die in the hurricane. Near misses, right?"

What could have happened suddenly doesn't count once the moment passes. Not good intentions or evil plans. Play the day, the moment, as it lays, not as what you should have or could have done. Jane-Claire smiles. Maybe Kit did teach a powerful lesson after all. A person must first endure.

"I have something for you." Jane-Claire pulls out the "I survived damn near everything" button that Kit gave her and pins it on the front of Mason's lab coat.

Mason had been holding his breath. He lets out a big sigh and laughs. "Where did you get this?"

Jane-Claire looks as mysterious as she can. "You don't want to know." She thinks of *Lord of the Rings* which is not a complete surprise, and specifically, a quote from Samwise, "But in the end, it's only a passing thing... this shadow. Even darkness must pass." And at that moment she knew with absolute certainty that she and her family didn't lose the most important thing.

BRIBERY IS the only way Jane-Claire coaxes Bituminous into a trip to Memaw's house, but super catnip treats eventually do the trick.

She carries the big black tomcat into Memaw's neighborhood, limping a little because her foot is pretty sore from the wood splinter gouge. She takes her time. The day is cool, crisp, and *Lord of the Rings* still plays in her thoughts. 'How can the end be happy? How can the world go back to the way it was when so much bad has happened?'

Jane-Claire has no idea except that they have to try.

Bituminous settles down by the time she closes in on Memaw's house. She holds the cat like a lump of coal and leans forward to whisper into his fight notched ears. "Don't say a thing. Remember, you promised."

Jane-Claire stands at the gate of the chain link fence surrounding Memaw's frame house then she hears the violin.

Faltering strains from Vivaldi, but the music is plain and sweet. She rushes through the front gate and up the porch steps but waits at the door.

She pushes into the door frame and slides down to sit on the porch, hold Bit, and listen to Natalie. For the first time in quite a while, she yearns for her video camera.

Memaw sneaks around from the back of the house and squats beside Jane-Claire. The old woman takes her hand and holds fast.

The longer they listen to the musical strains, the better and clearer the sound becomes. The violin is finally home.

When the Vivaldi concerto ceases, Memaw retreats.

Jane-Claire stands and knocks on the door. Natalie answers.

Today, she opens the door wide even if she still wears a tentative smile. "I sound terrible. I'm so out of practice."

"You sound great!" Jane-Claire hugs her and presses Bit between them. The cat meows in protest. Nat's eyes open. She stares, unwilling to believe her own sight.

Jane-Claire hugs Bit before offering him to Natalie.

She can resurrect a cat... just not Miss Shirin. The reunion is so bittersweet that Jane-Claire sheds tears that she thought she spent the night before.

Natalie and Jane-Claire sit on the porch swing. Natalie pets Bituminous who lounges against her like a pampered housecat rather than a feral hunter.

Memaw brings a tray of lemonade and special teacakes that she learned to make when she was a girl. The old woman smiles at Jane-Claire and nods.

Jane-Claire considers that a minor miracle in and of itself. She and Nat drink the home-brewed lemonade and nibble cookies on the first real day of autumn on the coast.

"We're having a 'Back to the Beach' bonfire tonight. You, Memaw, and anyone else you want to come are invited. Dad insists that we use the permit since it survived the storm. He says it's a sign, and the bonfire will signal a new beginning for the neighborhood, for the coast." Jane-Claire is thinking of funeral pyres.

"I don't know." Natalie shrugs. "Maybe. I haven't been..."

"You told me... It's hard. But come, Nat. Please." Jane-Claire can't believe how much she needs her there even if she doesn't understand how they can be celebrating with so much tragedy staring them in the face. Everyone's memories. So much is gone. Suddenly, Jane-Claire recalls Mrs.

Malbus and the Garth Run and how incredibly generous she was to share her story with her.

"Memaw says refrigerator trucks with bodies in them are parked down by the hospital." Natalie releases Bit who jumps to the floor, then up to the railing like a pro.

"What?" Natalie's statement comes out of the blue and proves more than Jane-Claire can bear. She jumps from the swing and paces the porch. "Why bring that up?"

Natalie shrugs. "I just wonder if it's true. I thought your dad might know."

"Dad says the coroner tries awfully hard to treat the dead with respect and to identify who they are." Jane-Claire says the spiel then clamps her mouth shut. If she says another thing, she'll say too much.

"Wait here a minute." Natalie scoops up Bituminous and carries him inside as if he'll disappear if she lets go of him. She retreats to the house and returns with Jane-Claire's journal, her video camera gadget bag, and the letters, now open. "I wrote the letters into your journal last night, so we both have copies."

Touched by her friend's gesture, Jane-Claire takes her journal that she thought was so important. "Well done, Nat. Thanks." She has everything she needs. . .. and more.

Nat embraces the big black tomcat. Her smile looks a little weird, as if she hasn't tried it on in a long time. "We'll come to the bonfire. I haven't been back to the beach because I guess, I was waiting for you."

"Well, I'm here, and I'm glad you are too." Jane-Claire pats Nat's shoulder. Emotion twists through her. She doesn't know what will happen in the future, whether she and Natalie will ever live close to each other again, but she believes that whenever they meet, they'll pick up right where they left off. The best of friends, no matter where life takes them.

"Mom and Lerue are driving down. He finished up his scholarship applications this morning, and Lerue would never miss a bonfire."

"Or any excuse to go to the beach." Natalie laughs and hugs Bituminous.

"That's true." Jane-Claire forces a smile.

LATE THAT AFTERNOON, Jane-Claire stands with her dad in front of their home on Second Street.

The white frame beach cottage looks shredded, like it was crushed between the fingers of a giant. The porch is gone along with the front bay window. Piles of debris surround the house. Glass glitters in the sandy landscape.

Jane-Claire's gratitude and sadness collide that day. The past, present, and future are too much to think of all at once. She surveys the scarred landscape. "Here at last, on the shores of the sea. It feels like a battleground, like Pelennor Fields."

Mason hugs her, "You saw it coming, Jane-Claire. Your eyes were open from the first." He holds a brown envelope in his left hand.

She wonders what it is and kicks at one of her old sandals, half - buried in the sand.

Mason points. "Hey, isn't that your flip flop?"

"One of them." Jane-Claire shrugs.

Mason opens his arms in a grand gesture encompassing the cement driveway, half covered with trash. "And I want to know… When are you going to learn to play that piano? The keys are right over there." He tries very hard to laugh.

White and black piano keys and all the piano's inside guts strewn all over the drive have a peculiar poignancy about them.

Jane-Claire shakes her head. Mom always says that dad has a sick gallows sense of humor because he went to medical school. Jane-Claire agrees. He is a little warped sometimes.

Mason takes hold of Jane-Claire's shoulders and turns serious. The sentiment is never far away. "Before everyone gets here... I got the initial coroner's report. The body's an elderly woman. I think perhaps Miss Adele, our recluse neighbor. It's not Nat's mom, that's for sure. I called a buddy of mine to check. Shirin is in Hattiesburg. She was pretty banged up. Severely depressed. Some people just shut down, J.C."

"Yeah, no kidding." Jane-Claire debates whether Natalie will make it to the beach tonight. The walk from Memaw's may be too far for her.

"But Shirin is getting better. She'll be able to come home soon." Her dad takes Jane-Claire's hand and squeezes.

Then Lerue booms in the distance, "This place is a hot mess. I can't even begin to skim. I thought they would've cleaned it up by now."

Mason and Jane-Claire separate. They wave to Lerue, who walks with Dona down Second Street.

Mason calls out to his son, "Looks better to me. At least they cleaned up the dead chickens."

"Land's valuable, the coast'll rebuild." Lerue, the eternal optimist.

"I don't know. Pappy's home in Long Beach was wiped out by Camille in '67. It's still an empty lot." Mason will always point out the place where Pappy had his summer home, every time he drives by on Beach Highway.

Jane-Claire runs to meet Dona, who gives her one of her looks. The one that says, "You have some explaining to do."

"Jane-Claire . . ." Her mom's voice makes her stop in her tracks.

She gives Dona her best chagrin. "Sometimes you just have to make your own decisions."

"Really? Imagine that." Dona nods. She understands.

They walk arm in arm to meet Mason in front of the house. Dona stops some distance before her husband, and the two of them square off like fighters.

But Mason came prepared. He pulls a battered wedding photo from the brown envelope and lifts it up in front of Dona, so she can see it.

"You were right. There's nothing here that can't be replaced. It's you and the kids I can't spare. Welcome home." That is all she needs to know. Dona and Mason embrace and kiss. When they come up for air, they show the photo to Lerue and Jane-Claire.

Jane-Claire sets her camera up and puts it on timer for another photo.

Standing in front of their destroyed home with big grins covering their faces, Dona, Mason, Lerue, and Jane-Claire wear mismatched clothes. Their hair is sweaty, disheveled. They look like clowns and the circus is catastrophe.

The only rule in an emergency is that there are no rules. Only a moral compass that for some stays straight, and for others, spins out of control.

Why the heck are they smiling?

Jane-Claire thinks you probably know.

The bonfire on the beach is superlative. Gulf water sparkles. Moonlight shines on the waves and sand. Tree trunks in the shallow water stick out at crazy angles and the heavy equipment used for sifting debris from the sand stand silent, like prehistoric dinosaurs.

Jane-Claire films the scene with her video camera

before she joins her mom, dad, and Lerue around the orange blaze.

As night settles, the bonfire grows brighter and brighter, and the sand is cool, even icy, absorbing any bit of body heat. They all stand close to each other and cling around the fire. Stars fill the inky black sky.

"My grace is sufficient for you. For my power is made perfect in weakness." In spite of everything, Jane-Claire and her family believe.

Natalie and Memaw come. Michael and his grandparents find their way.

All the Second Street neighbors circle the bonfire, drawn to the warmth and light. Jane-Claire thinks it's just kind of fun with everyone so close like that, and she sees what was saved, not what was lost. She'll take it, even for a moment.

Epilogue

Late August is a trigger that ignites hypervigilence in Jane-Claire. The month itself spawns anxiety without any provocation other than her own vivid memories.

She sits at a table across from Liz, a well-kept older woman, in the garden room of the "Authentic New Orleans style" restaurant.

Jane-Claire's back is straight as a board, her shoulders squared. Her long hair cascades from a center part. A dancer's posture is Jane-Claire's platform, and anyone can read the 'no' in her body language a mile away.

"It's been years since it happened." Liz leans forward across the white tablecloth and silver flatware that grace the table. "It's time."

"Time for what? Dredging up the past. Opening Pandora's box." Jane-Claire can't look her mother's best friend in the eye. Instead, she glances at her salad.

Chopped pickles lace a remoulade dressing that drenches boiled shrimp. Imagine. Where could the chef possibly be from? Definitely north of where the dish is done right.

Dona would have a fit. Her mom would also be upset that Liz's advice rankles Jane-Claire as much as the mess on her plate being passed off as Cajun Creole cuisine.

"Over twelve years have gone by." Liz's French heritage shines. She speaks with her hands, opening, closing, moving through the air to cajole and persuade.

Jane-Claire lets Liz's comment linger, uncontested.

After all, Liz did take time from her husband just out of the hospital from recent surgery and their eight grown children plus families to take her to lunch.

Liz has enough on her plate, all on her own. Jane-Claire watches her lift a spoon of soupy red beans and rice and grimace in disgust.

The statement sinks in. What can Jane-Claire say? How can she make Liz understand?

The passage of time makes no difference.

In truth, Jane-Claire has been writing about the hurricane ever since it happened. Small parts of her experience seep into suspense thrillers about attractive nuisances, mysteries about spectacular bluffs that win the game. She writes about secret anniversaries of the heart, murder by proxy and all of her work is colored by the toll of personal disaster.

Jane-Claire lives that story.

Liz may mean well by prodding her to write her "based on truth" experience but Jane-Claire can present the counter argument.

Tolkien didn't have first-hand knowledge of Hobbits, wizards, or "one ring to rule them all." He fought in World War I and that horror provided everything he needed.

"I don't want to... I can't." Jane-Claire's shoulders droop. Her voice is small.

She shoves the shrimp around her plate. Too much mayonnaise. Pickle bits. No Tabasco. The orange red dots of cayenne pepper look like tiny chiggers. The salad resembles vomit and she does not want to write reality.

"'I can't has no meaning for you. You can, and you know it." Liz is always so warm, caring. She has a lovely smile. Bull's-eye. She hit a nerve which is exactly what she intended. "Don't answer now. Just think about it. There've been so many natural disasters since…"

Jane-Claire gazes out the atrium window. Trees and vegetation in the Pacific Northwest appear foreign to her. She lives on a different coast now with a view of a vast, cold ocean. Her beach house is set high on a bluff. She bought the property, perceived as safe from Pacific whims, because it is not in a tsunami zone.

She remembers. Her home in Gulfport wasn't in a flood zone. The lawyers at the closing on that house laughed at her mother when she insisted on buying flood insurance.

An erratic wind blows through the restaurant garden.

Jane-Claire stands. The black linen napkin falls from her lap to the floor.

"Thank you, but I have to go. A storm's coming." Jane-Claire pictures her husband and daughter at home waiting for her.

"I believe in you." Liz continues to talk as Jane-Claire makes a beeline for the exit door of the restaurant. "Believe in yourself."

JANE-CLAIRE DRIVES the coast road a little too fast in her desperate rush to get home. Her thoughts race. Liz's suggestion startled her, every bit as much as the churning surf breaking on the wide Pacific beach.

Clouds come in from the west, dark and ominous. She

screeches onto her turnoff, pitching gravel as she maneuvers the car up the steep winding driveway.

Pulling into her garage, Jane-Claire flips the engine off and jumps from the car. But instead of going inside the house, she walks to the garage door opening and gazes out at the ocean.

Her hair lifts in the wind, streams behind her.

The farther Jane-Claire is from the storm, her storm, the less she wants to talk about it. She tries to forget, but the past is never past.

Disaster captures her. She sticks like glue to scenes of rising water. Horrific wind is a song. She has recurring dreams of inflatable plastic furniture that can be quickly blown up and put in place to furnish a room then just as quickly flattened to fit in an enormous suitcase in case she must respond to an evacuation order.

In her worst nightmares, she is drowning in debris filled storm surge. Disaster is intimate, palpable, smothering.

One set of ruins can't be compared to another. Shells, skeletons, and remnants are all individual. Body counts and property loss are not a true measure.

When the sky is blue again and the water, fire, shaking, or surge is gone, the scene is always familiar. Gray with a mottling of brown. Shades of shadow are the only color.

All aftermath looks pretty much the same.

Jane-Claire's husband bursts through the back door of their home. His smile says he's been waiting for her and that he is profoundly relieved that she is home.

Faye, their three year old daughter, wiggles and squirms in his arms.

As he sets her down in the garage, she breaks away and runs full tilt toward Jane-Claire. Daddy just misses grasping hold of Faye's dress.

"Mommy!" Arms outstretched, her little legs pump against the damp, slippery floor.

"Faye, slow down." Jane-Claire shouts, but warnings go unheeded, as always. She hurries to catch her.

But the little girl's desire to hug her mommy outweighs her ability to balance and she splats to the floor.

Faye cries. Her busted lip bleeds, swells.

Jane-Claire scoops Faye up into her arms. Blood flows down her chin and onto her arm.

Blood always looks like more than it really is. Jane-Claire hears her dad saying that as a caution not to panic. Although when she was young, Jane-Claire took it to mean that injury was of no consequence unless you were bleeding all over the floor.

Her dad didn't mean that at all.

"Shh, quiet now. Don't go on. It's not that bad. Just a little boo-boo." Jane-Claire holds her daughter tight as if she can absorb her distress. "Shush. Be quiet now. Calm down. Be a big girl."

Faye swallows her cries and stares at Jane-Claire. "But Mommy, it hurts." Blinking back tears and deadly serious, Faye tells her mommy that she is wrong.

Pain can't just be willed away because someone else wants it to stop.

"I know. I understand." Tears well in Jane-Claire's eyes. She hugs her little girl, pats her back.

Daddy brings a cloth with ice and holds it to Faye's lip.

Standing next to Jane-Claire, he puts his arm around her. Together, they stand at the garage entrance to watch the wind and waves crash as the storm barrels onshore.

About the Author

Dawn C. Crouch is a native of New Orleans and a former dancer with Houston Ballet. She holds a degree in Political Science, earned while teaching ballet at the University of Houston, pursued a graduate, and has written copy for a living.

She invites you to visit the Facebook page for her current project, DEAD CHILDREN'S PLAYGROUND, a supernatural thriller based on a Huntsville urban legend.

THE LAST PLAGUE, an eerily prescient tale of a serum that promises immortality but delivers a global pandemic is also available for pre-order.

In 2005, Hurricane Katrina blew Mrs. Crouch to Alabama where residing a safe distance from the beach, she works as a ballet instructor for Huntsville Ballet and Andalusia Ballet.

AGAINST THE WIND, a Young Adult catastrophe thriller, is based on the experience of her family during the storm. Mrs. Crouch can be contacted at dawn.crouch@gmail.com.

Made in the USA
Monee, IL
11 October 2020